KOH TABU

ANN KELLEY

OXFORD
UNIVERSITY PRESS

OXFORD
UNIVERSITY PRESS

Great Clarendon Street, Oxford OX2 6DP

Oxford University Press is a department of the University of Oxford.
It furthers the University's objective of excellence in research, scholarship,
and education by publishing worldwide in

Oxford   New York

Auckland   Cape Town   Dar es Salaam   Hong Kong   Karachi
Kuala Lumpur   Madrid   Melbourne   Mexico City   Nairobi
New Delhi   Shanghai   Taipei   Toronto

With offices in

Argentina   Austria   Brazil   Chile   Czech Republic   France   Greece
Guatemala   Hungary   Italy   Japan   Poland   Portugal   Singapore
South Korea   Switzerland   Thailand   Turkey   Ukraine   Vietnam

Oxford is a registered trade mark of Oxford University Press
in the UK and in certain other countries

First published 2010

British Library Cataloguing in Publication Data

Data available

ISBN: 978-0-19-275604-6

1 3 5 7 9 10 8 6 4 2

Printed in Great Britain by CPI Cox & Wyman, Reading, Berkshire

Paper used in the production of this book is a natural,
recyclable product made from wood grown in sustainable forests.
The manufacturing process conforms to the environmental
regulations of the country of origin.

TO THE REAL BONNIE

Acknowledgements

I have read, enjoyed and learned about the
natural history of Thailand and the islands in the
Gulf of Thailand, and about the habits of tigers
from these books:

Chasing the Dragon's Tail
Alan Rabinowitz, Anchor Books, Doubleday 1953;

The Singing Ape
Jeremy and Patricia Raemaekers, The Siam Society 1990;

Fight for the Tiger
Michael Day, Headline 1995;

Tigers in Red Weather
Ruth Padel, Little, Brown 2005

'When there is war, the poet lays down the lyre,
the lawyer his law reports, the schoolboy his books.'
                                    Mahatma Gandhi

'Where have all the flowers gone, long time passing?'
                                    Pete Seeger

Prologue

It all began with my mother changing her mind.
At the time I was glad that no grown-ups, except
Layla Campbell, were coming. Jas and I adored Layla
Campbell. We'd only met her three times, but we knew
that she was special, mysterious. She had taken over
as our cadet leader from Mrs O'Hanlon, who retired,
or went home or something.

Layla had this halo of curly red hair and wore
lots of black smudgy eye make-up, which made her
eyes glisten as if she was on the verge of tears.
She held a cigarette like Lauren Bacall in the
movies and had this big sad mouth. Jas and I called
her *the Duchess*, because of her posh Edinburgh
accent.

We tried to walk like her, stole cigarettes from
our mothers and choked trying to smoke like her. So
we couldn't have been happier that she was to lead
our camp.

But I'm going too fast. I'll start at the
beginning; go back to my journal. I remember when it
was new and pristine, with clean white pages and a
sky-blue hardback cover. Now it looks like the way
I feel — dirty, battered, torn, ripped, shattered,
falling apart.

My journal takes me back to the Forbidden Island
and it's all happening again . . .

CHAPTER ONE

Journal of Bonnie MacDonald
May 11th 1974
Amnuythip, Thailand.
Hooray! Tomorrow the Amelia Earhart Cadets go to the island
with Layla Campbell.

Senior Amelia Earhart Cadets:
Hope
May and Arlene (The Barbie Babes)
Jas
Me

Juniors:
Jody
Natalie
Sandy
Carly

To pack:
Journal
Waterproof holder for journal (v. important)
Sleeping bag
Torch (take lots of spare batteries)

Pencils
Rucksack
Book? Ask Mum for recommendation
Swiss Army knife
Change of clothes
Flip-flops
Towel
Toothbrush and wash things
Mozzie coil

Finally, we're off. It's bucketing down, the roads are flooded and you can hardly see out of the windscreen as there aren't any wipers, so the Duchess hangs out of the window and mops it with her tie-dyed scarf so the driver can navigate. She asks me to hold on to her legs so she doesn't fall out. She has these really long legs. Jas and I are laughing like mad.

The road disappears completely at one point and you can't tell where the ditches and fields begin. We're making a wake like a motorboat. People are wading through water to get home, their belongings in bundles on their heads. Only the gentle-faced water buffalo look unperturbed. They're in their element.

I glimpse through a gap in the frangipani trees a girl of about my age, her heart-shaped face made up like a woman's, scarlet lip colour, black eye kohl and powdered cheeks. Her black hair, decorated with red and orange flowers, is like a waterfall to her tiny waist. She stands on a balcony and looks as if she is waiting for someone to press a button so her life can begin.

Bar girls and their scrawny-legged bosses squat on tables

and look bored; Buddhist monks in orange robes hold umbrellas over their shaved heads, and confused pi-dogs swim around looking for a place to stand and bark at the suddenly wet world.

Inside the bus the juniors are shrieking and whooping every time the water gets really deep outside. There are stranded vehicles all over the place.

In the back of the bus, between bumps and careering, May is attempting to apply mascara to Arlene's eyelashes. They both turned up wearing no make-up but they have transformed themselves from senior cadets into *femmes fatales* in a matter of minutes, with bright pink lipstick and blue eye shadow. Arlene shrieks—a lump of mascara in her eye.

'Spider-eyes! You look like you've got spiders around your eyes!' May hitches up her boob tube and laughs.

Jas rolls her eyes at me.

Jody, Carly, and Sandy are staring out of the windows, clutching their teddy bears. It's their first camp. Carly and Sandy are the only ones wearing cadet uniform—khaki skirt and shirt, with a red neckerchief. Natalie is huddled in the corner looking anxious.

'Don't worry, Nat, we'll get through,' I tell her and she smiles faintly through her frown and carries on sucking the satin edge of her rag.

Sandy is the smallest girl, with pale hair and skin and skinny limbs. She looks as if she'd float away if you blew on her. Jas pulls her onto her lap so she doesn't get too bumped around on the bad roads.

The sun comes out by the time we're on the boat, but it's a rough trip and nearly everyone is sick. Not me, though.

5

Hope manages to vomit into the wind and gets it all over her orange sweatshirt.

'Are we there yet?' Sandy moans. She is as green as the praying mantis I found in my bedroom last week or one of the snakes the Thai boys torture on the compound.

The juniors' teddy bears are sodden.

An hour's boat trip is about as much as I can take at the best of times. The secret is to keep your eyes on the horizon so your brain can make sense of what is happening to your body. Daddy told me that. He used to vomit in his helmet when he first started flying. Now he flies Phantom F4s. He's in the Special Air Services Regiment deployed as an instructor to the United States Air Force front-line base at Utapao, an hour's drive away from our home compound at Amnuythip. Before that he was an instructor in Borneo in the war against Sukarno.

We've been in Thailand for two years. We don't see much of him; he mostly has to stay on the base, and when we do see him he looks very tired with dark bags under his eyes, and his wavy brown hair has gone completely grey. But he's still handsome. These days he has a very short fuse, and I mostly stay out of his way. Mum says that's wisest. Daddy reckons the war will be over in less than a year. We'll go back to Scotland then.

It'll be great seeing Grandpa and Grandma again, but it will be hard leaving friends here and I do love Thai food, especially sticky rice. There's a little beach bar at Amnuythip where they have the best sticky rice ever. We have parties there sometimes when Daddy and the other fathers are home. The Buddhist bar owner was a monk for many years and he's covered in tiny tattoos, mostly words, like a newspaper of flesh. He and his wife cook chicken, pork, prawns, stalked barnacles, clams, lobster and rice stick noodles with all sorts of herbs and spices—ginger, coriander, lemongrass and galangal. They were childhood sweethearts and lost touch with each other for years, but met again when she was a widow with five children. Mum thinks that's so romantic. I remember one evening when we were all there having fun and the parents were drinking beer and laughing, a Thai man on the beach shot himself in the foot. He was very drunk and probably didn't feel a thing, Mum said.

There's a tiny part of me that wishes Mum were here. Mrs Campbell smiles and hugs the little ones, but I can tell that's she's worried. The boat bumps and shudders on the waves.

We're nearing the island when the outboard motor stutters and stops.

'What's up?'

'Are we out of fuel?'

The boat is drifting side-on to the waves, which makes it plunge sickeningly. The boatman, who looks about a hundred years old, can't get the motor started. He only has one eye, like the guard's wife in our compound. Her eye socket is stuffed with cotton waste and the boatman's is covered with a black patch like a pirate.

'Isn't *that* where we are supposed to be going, Mrs Campbell? We've gone too far.' I point to the landing place we came to last time we camped.

The sea sweeps us quickly past the island and we seem to be drifting fast. The current is really strong.

'I'm sure the boatman knows what he's doing, Bonnie.'

We watch him doing things to the outboard motor but it still won't start. We've gone way past our little island, and lots of others too. They rise like big lush anthills straight out of the water.

The boatman hauls up a small canvas sail and gabbles at us. I don't know what he's saying but the Duchess translates.

Rather than tack back against the wind and current to our island, which will take hours, she explains, he's taking us to another, which is much bigger than the one we had planned to camp on, but has a landing place and fresh water, he says. Or that's what Mrs Campbell reckons he says. Is her Thai really that good? I'm impressed. But the others are appalled.

'There are over fifty islands in this archipelago,' shouts Mrs Campbell between screams and groans.

'I don't care where we stop as long as it's soon,' I tell Jas. She nods wearily and we huddle closer together. Waves crash over us and the boat is nearly swamped a couple of times. We use our hands to bail out.

'Where are the lifebelts? No lifebelts? No, of course not. Why did I ever say yes to this stupid trip?'

'Shut up, Spider-eyes, will you just shut up!'

The Barbie Babes (Jas and I thought of that name) squabble at the best of times. And this is not the best of times.

We are getting very close to a reef. Waves build up into breaking surf and our boatman steers carefully towards a gap between two exposed rocks and coral heads. As the boat reaches the gap it is raised high on a wave and we are swept into a lagoon.

There is a thin stretch of sand and, on the right, black rocks reaching out into the sea, like a natural harbour, except that as we get closer we can see that waves are surging between the rocks, making it dangerous to get too close.

Another wave surfs us in to land safely on a steeply sloping beach. As quickly as we can, we lift the little girls over the side and help Mrs Campbell unload the tents and bags and boxes of provisions. She gives me her guitar to carry.

'Oh, solid land!' Arlene sinks to her knees and kisses the sand. Then splutters and spits. Anything to avoid helping.

Jas, Hope, and I run back and forth, carrying the rucksacks and provisions. The water swirls around us and the boat twists in the restless waters.

For some reason the boatman won't put his feet on the island. Mrs Campbell tries to get him to help unload the crates of bottled water but he shakes his head, yelling, 'Yaksha! Yaksha! Koh Tabu!' and keeps pointing back to the mainland.

It takes all our strength to pull the crates ashore. Mrs Campbell beckons the others to help shove the boat off the beach and the boatman doesn't even wave as he turns towards the sea. He gives up trying to get the outboard going and sails now for the mainland, after a difficult launch over the surf. We won't see him until he picks us up in three days' time.

'What was he saying, Mrs Campbell?'

'Nothing, Bonnie. A silly taboo. The locals don't come here if they can help it.'

'Why don't they?'

'He didn't say. It's only superstition, whatever it is.'

'What's Yaksha?'

9

'I think it's something to do with Hindu gods, isn't it? A temple guardian?' says Jas.

'Giant. A mythical giant,' murmurs Mrs Campbell.

I feel as if we are still rising and plunging on the waves and eventually have to sit down while my head settles.

'I'm going to explore.'

'No, not yet, May, we need to set up camp first. Then you can search for wood for a camp fire.' Mrs Campbell slaps May's bottom with the flat of her hand and May shrieks, laughing. Everyone smiles, relieved to be together and safe.

It's paradise, no adults to spoil things. I don't count the Duchess as an adult. She's fun. I look around, making mental notes for my journal. There are wispy casuarinas and tall coconut palms at the top of the beach and green jungle rising steeply in a backdrop. The pale strip of beach is nearly covered by water, and there's all sorts of flotsam and jetsam on the tide line. Treasures to take home and to write about in my journal.

Most of us wanted to pitch camp under a banyan tree— beneath its spreading branches. But Jas insisted it was bad luck to sleep under a banyan—something about ghosts and demons living in the branches.

So we end up choosing a clear space near the banyan, above the high tide mark.

It's hard work pitching our tent but great fun. The wind keeps whipping it away from us, and Jas and I laugh hysterically, almost wetting ourselves. I'm glad Jas is with me and also pleased Mum didn't come now. She'd have complained about the primitive sleeping arrangements and refused to use the latrine, which we seniors have dug well away from the camp.

We drape mosquito nets over our sleeping bags, though it must be too windy for mozzies. I can save my mosquito coil for another night. I love the way the burnt embers look like a dead, desiccated, curled-up snake in the morning.

The Duchess unpacks our Thai cooker, a simple barbecue with a lid on it, places the charcoal inside and lights it now so it will be good and hot for cooking our supper.

'Now you can look for firewood, but don't stray far from the beach, please, girls, and keep an eye on the wee girls.'

She means the juniors. In Amelia Earhart Cadets we have seniors (14 to 17 years) and junior members (between 9 and 13 years). You can become a chief cadet if you pass ten tests with credit. I have only passed five so far: First Aid; Knots; Woodwork; Swimming; Navigation. I haven't been a cadet for very long. The only chief cadet among us is Jas, who, like me, is fourteen. She's brilliant at everything, but you can't feel envious or cross about it because she is so sweet natured. She's the sort of girl who would give you her last square of chocolate; she doesn't gossip and she can keep a secret. That's rare.

We all walk along the narrow strip of white sand, gathering shells and driftwood. There are striped tiger cowries and fragments of oyster, cone shells, and pink tellins, like a baby's fingernails. We don't get these on the beach at Amnuythip. There's nothing on the sand there apart from filter tips and prawn shells.

The wind drives fine grains of sand into our eyes and forces the waves far up the beach, sending spume flying like soap suds through the air. Still, I find so many lovely shells I can't carry them all. And there's plenty of driftwood and huge chunks of chestnut-coloured kelp dragged up from the deep. We end up with quite a pile of wood to keep the fire going and Mrs Campbell is delighted.

'We've brought plenty of charcoal,' she says, 'but there's nothing quite like a wood fire.'

She says we should map the island while we're here and invent names for the beaches and landmarks. That's our only task apart from keeping a journal, which I do anyway. I write all sorts of things in my journal—like love poems to Lan Kua, which I've never shown him, of course. Lan Kua says I am *Pee Prai*—a beautiful woman spirit who entices men to fall in love with her. He's such a charmer, and I am not a flirt. I like to sketch in my journal and stick found things into it, like interesting matchbox covers, leaves and flowers, Thai labels, feathers and photographs, stuff from magazines that I don't want to lose, and other poems that I write that are fit to be seen by the general public—unlike the love poems.

We explore the beach, which I have named Landing Place. At one point there's no sand, only jagged rocks that rise to a peak about fifty feet high, so we have to clamber over those at sea level. I've named that Dragon Point, because that's what it looks like, the tail pointing into the sea, the large head facing inland. Hope points out a shallow cave looking over the tail. She has to shout above the noise of the wind. We only cover a tiny part of the island's circumference, I reckon, but we'll do some more tomorrow. It's much bigger than the island we were supposed to have camped on. But this one is definitely more interesting. And if it has fresh water why isn't it inhabited? That's the kind of thing my dad would think about if he was here.

We head back towards the camp.

The little kids are paddling, running in and out of the swooshing waves as they run up the steep beach. I sit down to watch the tiny bubble crabs organize grains of sand into balls. I could watch them for ever. Ghost crabs run towards the sea and get swept back by waves. Sea birds scream and whirl in the wind.

Sandy calls in a thin high voice, 'Hi, Bonnie, aren't you coming in?' She looks like lots of white-skinned kids who live in the tropics—pale with dark bags under her eyes. There's no sun, just low grey clouds, so she won't burn anyway. Mum says I'm lucky. My skin tans easily and I love the heat and sun.

'Don't swim just here, kids, there's a rip, by the look of it.' I have learned to read the sea from my grandfather in Scotland. He's a good fisherman. I'm not much good but he says he's going to teach me one day, when we go back to live nearby.

'A rip?' shouts Arlene. 'What's that when it's at home?'

'It's a sort of surge of water going from the shore to the sea: a very strong current. Don't go too far,' I call. But they are too scared to come to harm, which is good.

They screech with excitement as each wave threatens to grab them by the ankles and carry them off.

'You are such a know-all, Bonnie MacDonald.' Arlene pokes out her tongue. I ignore her. I know what I'm talking about.

'And you are such a know-nothing, Arlene Spider-eyes,' shouts May. Arlene hurls herself at May, who shrieks, splashing and laughing.

Huge dark clouds growl, and for a moment the sea looks as if it will engulf us all. Colours are somehow brighter,

13

more vivid, held in by the strange thick ceiling of green-grey. It's wonderful sitting here, watching, I feel so alive. Here we are on our very own desert island: nine of us, and Layla Campbell. It's like the best adventure we could possibly have.

May, Arlene, and Hope have been rummaging in the boxes of equipment and go fishing in a large rocky pool near the shore with a fishing net taped on the end of a bamboo pole and a hand-held fishing line. Or rather, Hope fishes and the Barbie Babes sit and watch and make stupid comments. Hope falls in up to her shoulders, which is pretty deep as she's really tall, and loses a flip-flop and her glasses. They spend more time fishing for her glasses than for anything edible but bring back some little silver fish, which we'll cook later.

The juniors have claimed their own private playground under the banyan. The hundreds of roots growing down from branches act as props and form arches and passageways, and the girls run in and out of them and swing from them. They're having the time of their lives.

Jas says banyans are sacred to Hindus and Buddhists and represent eternal life.

'I thought you said there are bad spirits in them?'

Jas shrugs. 'There's good and bad spirits everywhere.' She's very knowledgeable about Thailand. Her mother runs a 'Get to Know the Locals' group and she invites people to come to talk to them about Hindu and Buddhist customs. I get all my local knowledge from Lan Kua who has made it his job to educate me. He teaches me naughty words in Thai and when I say them he screams with laughter and does handstands on the balcony rails of our house. He's good fun. Dad doesn't approve of him.

Mrs Campbell has been working hard and as the light fades we eat hamburger with buns, and Hope's delicious little fish. Then we toast marshmallows and sing songs around our campfire, red sparks flying into the black sky like fireflies. Mrs Campbell pulls out her guitar, and plucks the strings. She looks every bit the Duchess and Jas and I smile at each other, knowing we're both thinking the same.

'What's that tune?'

'*Don't care if it rains or freezes,*

'*long as I got my plastic Jesus . . . '*

'Oh yeah, *Cool Hand Luke.* I *lurv* Paul Newman.'

'Yeah, those gorgeous blue eyes.' May flutters her eyelashes.

The Duchess carries on with the thin tune Paul Newman played on the banjo in the movie when he heard his mother had died.

'Time to turn in now, you young ones,' she says as she ends the song, but we're all having too much fun and Jody, Sandy, Natalie, and Carly ignore her, getting up and running down to the sea to whoop and screech, jumping away from the rushing waves. Even scaredy-cat Natalie is joining in, though she's taken her comfort rag with her.

'"What we have here is a failure to communicate,"' quotes Jas, speaking in a nasal drawl like the prison boss in *Cool Hand Luke,* and I laugh.

'Sing that song you made up, Bonz,' Jas urges me.

'You write songs?' Mrs Campbell's eyes light up and she smiles at me.

'No, not really. Poems.'

'Poems? I love poetry. You must read me your poems sometime.'

I'm glad it's dark as I can feel my cheeks redden with pleasure.

Then the Duchess strums and sings sweetly:

'*Where have all the flowers gone,*

Long time passing?'

'It's a beautifully sad song,' I say.

'It's an anti-war song, Bonnie. Did you know that?' she asks.

'You're not anti-war are you, Mrs Campbell?'

'A rather unorthodox and dangerous thing to be if you live on a US military base in wartime, don't you think?'

'I guess.' She didn't answer my question.

The Duchess sings again.

'You have a lovely voice, Mrs Campbell,' says Jas.

'Oh no, Jasmine.' Suddenly her laugh has no humour. 'My husband . . . ' Her voice cracks, 'My husband was a *true* musician.' She strums a few chords and bends her head, a curtain of auburn hair covering her face. Without saying any more we follow the juniors away down the beach into the shadows, to leave her to her thoughts.

We play tag, running in and out of the darkness, chasing each other and squealing with pretend terror. The wind sweeps our voices away. Hope gives the juniors towel rides. They love it, even Natalie. They are like little monkeys climbing all over her. I look back and watch the Duchess as she lies by the fire, smoking, drinking from a bottle. She looks so romantic in her ankle length antique petticoat with lace around the hem. It's dyed a bright crimson, and

16

with it she wears an embroidered white peasant blouse with ribbon threaded around the loose neck. She has such style, the Duchess; she looks so unusual, so individual.

'Have you noticed she isn't wearing a bra?' Arlene whispers loudly to May.

'Yeah, so what? Her tits are bigger and perkier than yours.'

'Are not.'

'Are.'

'Are not.'

Arlene pushes May over sideways and May pushes her back and they both giggle. Jody's pleading voice interrupts their bickering. 'Mikey says can we stay here for ever?'

'Who the hell's Mikey?' Arlene asks.

'Her imaginary friend. Yes, Jody, if you like. We'll join the monkeys and gibbons in the trees and eat fruit and leaves.' I quite like the idea of living on a desert island. Though I could do without Arlene and May.

There are no stars tonight and the wind has worsened, or improved, depending on your point of view. If I were the wind I would want to go faster and faster and whip the trees and push houses over just to show how strong I was. So, the wind has actually improved her performance, not worsened it.

And if the sea feels things too, maybe he wants to get higher and fiercer too, hooliganizing the shore. Perhaps all the elements are fighting for supremacy, determined to be the most powerful force.

I'm dizzy on cola and fresh air and excitement. The juniors are rubbing their eyes from tiredness and the smoke. The occasional bright star exposes itself between clouds, but then the sky descends, dropping rain from its blackness. It drives towards us in sheets across the sea and we flee, laughing, to our tents.

Tucked into our sleeping bags I read aloud to Jas from the book I brought with me—*Zen and the Art of Motorcycle Maintenance* by Robert M. Pirsig. It's a little soggy around the edges but not too bad. Mum's just read it and says it's interesting and adult, and it's a cult classic and it's about time I read something intelligent and challenging. She's always got her head in a book. It really annoys Dad. I'm more of a physical person, like him. I like to be doing things rather than reading about them.

'Give it a go, you'll like it,' she said. So I'm trying to read it, but it's hard work. I find it's easier to understand if I read it out loud.

'*Everything gets written down, formally, so that you know at all times where you are, where you've been, where you're going and where you want to get. . . . Sometimes just the act of writing down the problems straightens out your head as to what they really are.*' In the book he's talking about fixing the bike, but I think that advice applies to lots of problems. I'm always writing down my problems—like— if Lan Kua wanted to kiss me, would I say yes? My journal knows all my secrets.

'Do you think Lan Kua is serious about me?' I ask Jas.

She knows how keen I am on Lan Kua.

'Yeah, sure he is and he's cute, but not good enough for you.'

'He's going to be a monk soon,' I tell her.

'I thought he wanted to be a kick boxer.'

'Yeah, he does, but it's something most Thai boys do,

you know? Like a rite of passage or something. He was ordained last year, and he has to spend time as a monk to gain merit for his family.'

The canvas billows like a sail on a yacht.

'Weird. Will he be allowed to have sex?'

'Jas! Stop it.' We hit each other, giggling.

'Time to settle down now,' Mrs Campbell calls to us above the noise of the wind and the tents. 'It's been a long day for us all.'

I unwrap my journal and write in it quickly. I couldn't possibly stay awake long enough to write about everything that's happened today.

12th May Day 1 on the island, 11 p.m.
Wonderful day, wonderful island—THE WRONG ISLAND, but who cares! Paradise.
But it sure is windy!

I slip the book and journal back inside the waterproof folder and tuck it inside my sleeping bag against my leg. Jas is breathing as if she's already asleep. I check that my sneakers are close by—have to wear them so we don't get the dreaded chiggers (pesky critters, they are such small mites you can hardly see them, but they cause such discomfort)—before I switch off my torch, which I've looped around my wrist.

CHAPTER TWO

'Help! Help! Oh my God! What's happening? *Help!*'

'What is it? *Flashlight!* Where's the torch? Got it!'

Screams. Breath torn from my chest.

'Oh God, the tent! *The tent!*'

'Grab it, hang *on!*'

'Too strong!'

The wind, like some fierce horned beast, rips our tent to shreds. Its vicious roar deafens us as we're blasted awake. One moment we're snug in our sleeping bags and the next we're totally exposed to the elements. Jas and I laugh at first, then realize the enormity of what's happening. It's not just us. All the other tents are blowing away too. We grab at the flimsy stuff and try to hold it down, but it's useless, torn canvas flies away like a huge freed bird, high into the furious sky. We're immediately soaked and chilled. We hang on to each other, buffeted by gusts that take away my breath. It feels as if my eyes are being torn out.

'Girls, where *are* you? Oh God . . . '

Then comes an enormous terrifying blast of air, an explosion that takes the last of our tents, leaving us like hermit crabs without a shell. A livid, full red moon briefly illuminates them, turning them into dragons as they are whisked away to disappear into the terrible night.

Cries are whipped away from our lips. The wind snarls and tall waves crash close. Sheet lightning lights up the sky all around. In one flash I see girls etched against the white surf, heads forward, bodies leaning, tilted into the teeth of the wind as if frozen. I see a sleeping bag rolling along the top of the beach and wrapping itself around a palm tree.

'Oh, *help*! No, no, no!'

'Teddy, my *tedd*—'

'We're going to die. Mummy, Mummy . . . *Mummy*. Please . . .'

Screams. Moans. Screams. Soundless sobbing and wailing and calls for help lost in the awesome howl of the wind. It must be a hurricane. It's chaotic, a disaster. Like a terrible dream. Jas and I try to move towards the others. Sand in my eyes, mouth, I'm breathing sand. I'm choking. My hair feels as though it's being ripped from my scalp. The wind is attacking us as if it bears a grudge.

'Hang . . . to . . . wee ones, *hang on* . . . sleeping bags,' shouts Mrs Campbell, her words whipped away into the night as soon as they leave her lips, and we do, except that we can't see who's who except when lightning splits the sky. I crawl on all fours with Carly, I think, in my grasp, away from the waves, towards trees, which are being flung and torn as we are. The wind snatches at our sleeping bags, but we hang on, grimly.

A sudden dreadful racket of cawing and screeching, and I see in another flash a black mass of birds—like a flock of mad witches, upside down, flying backwards, inside out, in a dense fast-moving cloud. Fork lightning strikes a tall tree only twenty feet away and it explodes before our

21

eyes: twelve-foot splinters, like flame-throwers, are hurled into the sea and all around us. We throw ourselves onto the sand and instinctively cover our heads. Close by on the sand a burning splinter glows and blackens. A huge gleaming branch gallops along the beach spitting blue flames. I can't stop shaking. It's like war, I think, like being a Vietnamese peasant when a bomb drops, maybe dropped by someone I know.

I cling to the trunk of the nearest palm with one arm, the other curled around Carly, who is blown so hard by the wind that I have difficulty keeping hold of her. She loses her sleeping bag; it is torn from her grip and bounces along the shore like a fat acrobat, eventually disappearing into the forest. We crouch together, blinded by sand and wind. The sea is too close but I dare not let go to move further back into the trees. The palm that is our anchor is blown so far over that the feathered branches are furiously sweeping the sand like a mad robotic broom. In the brief instances of intense light I can see the fringe of palms all along the beach bent almost horizontal.

It's 3 a.m., my green-eyed watch tells me, and still the wind moans and screeches.

It's like the end of the world.

'Bon . . . ? *Bonnie* . . . ?'

'Here, Jas, with Carly,' I yell to her—can't see her, but she's somewhere close. I can't let go of either the trunk or Carly to switch on my torch. I hear the low wail of children, helpless and frail: or is it me, my own terror?

In a lull, which is somehow terrifying, as if the wind is taking a big breath to blow even harder, we manage to crawl along the beach, moving from tree to tree, rock to rock, and stumbling over fallen trunks and the tumbling casuarina branches. Rain and sea spray whip me, snot smears my hair; my legs are clawed and spat at by sand and flying debris.

I open my eyes as little as possible, only to keep track of the crawling bodies ahead of us. I notice, like a fussing mother, most of us have managed to save our shoes.

Finally, at the far end of the beach, clambering over and above the rocks where the Dragon's Tail curves out into the sea, we find shelter in the shallow cave Hope saw yesterday. It's more like the armpit of an overhanging rock. Too exhausted to speak, we shiver and tremble in a terrified huddle. Later, the fearsome wind returns with increased power and we cling even more closely together, high above where the white surf crashes, though the spume flies over us and settles on our clothes and the cave floor.

The terrible rage and whine of the storm is inside my head, in my brain, cutting out all rational thought. Wet through, cold, frightened beyond anything in my experience, sand in every orifice, I give up and simply endure.

We huddle in wet, sandy sleeping bags. Carly shares mine, sobbing against me. The juniors are beyond comforting, curled up like caterpillars. They stink of urine and wet hair. Jas nudges at me and points to where we can see waves reaching right up beyond the tree line.

I have no sense of the passage of time, but eventually, a faint streak of sickly saffron light appears on the horizon. Low dark clouds hang ragged in a lurid green sky. Mrs Campbell crawls around us checking to see if there are any injuries.

We begin to talk to one another, hushed and shocked. Mrs Campbell does a roll call.

'Jasmine?'

'Yes, I'm here. Wish I wasn't, but I am.'

'Bonnie?'

'Yes.' I am attempting to get rid of the sand in my ears and nose and the corners of my eyes.

'May?'

'Here, Mrs Campbell, and I'm covered in cuts and scratches.'

'Hope?'

Hope snivels and mumbles, 'Uh ha.'

'Arlene?'

'Yeah, bad luck.'

'Natalie?'

'My leg, my leg.' She's been whimpering all night, come to think of it.

'We'll have a look at it in a minute, dear.'

'Jody?'

'Yes, Mrs Campbell.'

'Carly?'

Carly sobs a small 'Yes,' then wails, 'Teddy, teddy!' But Mrs Campbell doesn't respond.

'Sandy?' she calls next.

Silence.

'Sandy? Sandy? *Where's Sandy?*'

We look around us.

'Carly, where's your sister, dear?'

Carly cries, low and persistently.

'What is it, dear? Where *is* Sandy?'

'I don't know, I don't know.'

24

'What do you mean? You haven't seen her?'

'I don't know.' Carly sobs loudly into my arms, snot streaking her pale little moon face. I shake my head at Mrs Campbell.

'Sandy! Sandy! Sandy!'

'You had her, didn't you?' Arlene asks May.

'No, thought you had her.'

A memory jolts me into words.

'Sleeping bag. Saw it over there, blown along. Empty . . . thought it was empty.' The image of the windblown bag is as clear to me as if it were happening now. I pass Carly's limp body to Hope, who draws her close.

Three of us—Mrs Campbell, Jas, and I—crawl along the top of the beach, from tree to tree, our eyes half closed against the flying sand, to where the sleeping bag is practically buried at the foot of a palm.

'Is she alive? Oh my God, is she breathing?'

'I don't know, give me room.'

'Her head, the blood . . . '

'Oh no, oh God!'

Mrs Campbell lays her fingers against Sandy's neck.

'She's dead. She must have hit her head on the tree trunk.'

I can't believe it. It's not happening. It can't be happening.

Jasmine and I cling to each other in horror. Mrs Campbell is crying and breathing strangely.

'What are we going to do, Mrs Campbell?'

'I don't know, I really don't know.'

Sand is creeping over the little girl's face as we watch.

Mrs Campbell suddenly pulls the zip up over Sandy's bloody head and beckons us to follow her back to the shelter. She gathers the older girls together and tells them the terrible news.

'She's dead, she's dead!' May starts screaming, and Mrs Campbell slaps her on the cheek, but not before Carly gets the message.

The little girl tries to go to where her sister lies but Mrs Campbell grabs her and hugs her tightly.

'No, don't look, don't look.'

Carly doesn't cry, she just closes her eyes, her mouth a thin straight line, and curls up in Mrs Campbell's arms.

CHAPTER THREE

13th May
Morning, Day 2 on the island
We've survived. But last night was the worst night of my life.
Sandy is dead.

I can't believe I'm writing these words. There was a terrible
storm and now Sandy is dead. Mrs Campbell says we have to
keep calm.

I wish Mum was here. I wish she hadn't changed her mind
about coming.

I try to think back to the day before yesterday. To a normal
life.

'Bonnie, Sweetie, *Bonz* . . . where are you?'

'Hi, Mum, I'm here.' I'm sitting on the wooden steps of
Lek's house, in the shade of a huge fig tree, trying out my Thai
with her son, Lan Kua, who is sixteen and drop dead gorgeous.
Her four other little children, all with talcum powdered round
cheeks, are giggling and pushing each other off the steps.

It's a hot sticky day, hotter even than usual, and very still,
the air full of the smell of burning charcoal and a sickly
scent of rotting lotus blossoms.

One of Lek's kids is poking at an ants' nest under the tangling roots of the tree. Lan Kua takes his stick away. The five year old looks astonished.

'There you are! Hi, kids! *Sawat dit!*' Mum's wearing white baggy shorts and a black vest, flip-flops and big sunglasses and she's fanning herself with a folded magazine. Her face is shiny with perspiration. She sits next to me on the step.

'Bonz, do you mind if I don't come on the island trip, Sweets?'

'No, that's OK with me.'

'Sure? Only you know I get seasick in a rowing boat even, and anyway,' she stands and shimmies her feet in the sandy earth, wiggling her hips, 'I've had an invitation to a party at the base.' In front of Lan Kua! I'm so embarrassed. She's forty, for goodness' sake.

'I'm cool, Mum.' I wish she'd go and leave me in peace.

'OK, I'll let your Mrs Campbell know. She's perfectly able to look after you all, I'm sure.'

'Yes.' I want Lan Kua to know that this isn't some silly girls' outing that I'm going on. 'Mrs Campbell's keen on survival in the wilderness, and all that sort of thing.'

'Well, I hardly think survival skills will be necessary. You're only going for three nights.' Mum laughs and lights a cigarette. 'Lemonade's ready, dear, are you coming?'

'Lemonade's for kids, Mum. Mrs Campbell says that English tea's the thing. Earl Grey would be delightful.' Hey, I sound exactly like her. She's originally Scottish, from Edinburgh, like us, but lived in England for a while and knew the Beatles and the Rolling Stones. She's going to teach me how to play the guitar.

'Hmm, Earl Grey tea and survival don't seem to go together somehow.'

'Mum, she's a civilized survivor.' Mrs Campbell—Layla— is in her mid-twenties, and I don't think Mum likes her very much. She's very pretty, with curly dark red-brown hair to her shoulderblades, fair skin and brown eyes. She lives in Pattaya, which Mum says is a glorified brothel, as it's an R and R destination for US troops and I'm not allowed to go there without her or Dad. We've only met her a few times. She couldn't be more different from Mrs O'Hanlon.

I overheard Mum and her gossipy friends talking about Mrs Campbell last week. They were being bitchy about her because she was married to an American flyer who died in enemy action last year and now it is said that she is being 'kept' by a senior member of staff. Whatever that means.

'She should have been sent back stateside long ago,' I heard one of them say. Then someone called her 'a clever survivor'. I expect that's how she got to be cadet leader.

I feel sorry for her. Fancy the man you love dying a year or so after you marry him! They're jealous because she's young and pretty. Jas and I love her.

'Hi, Bonn, you ready for a trip to Paradise?' It's my best friend Jas.

Jas makes me laugh. Everything is a laugh with her around. Like my dad, her dad is in the USAF at Utapao. He's a colonel. Our maid Lek is married to their cook.

Jas has Jody and Natalie in tow, as usual. Jody is her shadow and Natalie is Jody's little sister. Jas is so pretty she attracts people to her as if she's a movie star. She has a permanent tan and a figure to die for. She's only my age but she looks sixteen. I'm taller but my figure is straight up and down, no bust as yet, just buds. Mum says I shouldn't worry, she was the same and clothes hang better from a flat chest. I'm not interested in clothes. I live in shorts, T-shirt, and flip-flops. Should have been a boy, Mum says. She bought me a dress—blue 'to match my eyes'—for my birthday, but I've worn it only once, to a Thanksgiving dinner at the base.

Jas carries her baby brother on one hip. Her mother gets these really bad migraines and has to lie in a darkened room for days. She can't even stand the sound of the ceiling fan.

'Yeah, I'm ready. You?'

'Yeah . . . got my new flashlight, sleeping bag . . . not sure what book I'm taking.'

'I've got something you might like,' Mum says to me.

'Mikey's coming,' Jody interrupts.

'Sure he is.' Jas knows about Jody's imaginary friend and humours her.

Natalie is quiet. She's a timid child: scared of the guard with one leg; scared of his one-eyed wife; scared of the scabby dogs that roam the beach; scared of her own shadow. She's nine but acts younger: sucks her thumb and drags a scraggy piece of blanket with her wherever she goes. Their mother shouts at them a lot. I think she's too young to be away from home for three nights, but maybe she'll enjoy it.

'What does Mikey look like?' I ask Jody.

'Don't be silly, you can see what he looks like.' She points vaguely to one side and smiles at her invisible pal.

'Oh OK, yeah, aren't I stupid!'

Jas and I giggle.

'Come on, gang.' Mum picks up Lan Kua's three-year-old sister, and the other white-cheeked cherubs follow us, chanting, 'Leem-on-ay, leem-on-ay leem-on-ay . . . '

I chant, 'Earl Grey tea, Earl Grey tea, Earl Grey tea . . . '

Jas takes Jody and Natalie (and Mikey, presumably) back to their mum, who is wandering around their yard in her tatty dressing gown and curlers. She's a birdbrain and an airhead, Mum says, but she feels sorry for her as her husband is such a creep.

Jas lives in the big house at the back of the compound with her mum and dad, when he's there, and her baby brother Francisco. He's gorgeous. Mum says she could eat him. I think she'd like another baby but she's too old, probably.

'See you later, alligator,' Jas calls.

'In a while, crocodile,' I reply.

That night after supper Jas comes over as usual. I have the ceiling fan on full making the pale blue cotton curtains dance over the screen windows. Green geckos wait patiently on the ceiling and walls for passing insects. The first time I saw one I thought it was a plastic toy. Jas says they have these amazing suckers on their footpads that allow them to walk up and down anything including mirrors and glass, and upside down.

We lie on my bed and listen to the night—the patter of small lapping waves on the beach beyond over the dirt road, the shrill squeak of cicadas, the big tokay lizards calling. They usually repeat their call three or four times, but tonight one repeats the metallic song, *tokay . . . tokay . . . tokay . . . tokay . . . tokay.*

31

'Did you hear that? Five times. That's bad luck. It means death.'

'Yeah, death for a mouse,' I say and laugh. I'm not superstitious.

'Who's all coming on the trip?'

'Well, not my mum.'

'Yeah, shame. I like your mom.'

'It doesn't matter. There's only four juniors—Jody, Natalie, Sandy, and Carly, and us seniors—Hope, Arlene, May, you and me. Should be great.'

'Arlene and May! Oh my God!'

'Yeah, I know, they're complete thickos. But we'll have each other.'

'What do you think of Hope?'

'I feel sorry for her, kind of. Her father is an arsehole.' Mum would hate me using that word.

'Uncouth.'

'Definitely.'

'A grunt, even.'

'Yeah.'

'And she looks very like him, doesn't she? She's got so little going for her.'

'We'll be extra nice to her.'

'OK.'

'Who'll she share a tent with?'

'Don't look at me! I'm not going to be *that* nice!'

13th May 74 The island, later in the day
I must record in my journal everything that is happening to us. I need to remember it all as clearly as possible. So much is

happening and my head is in a whirl and hurts. Don't know how I hurt it—a branch? Or did I fall and bang it on a rock? It was all so confusing and chaotic.

The gale has eased a little but not much, though the wind doesn't sound so awful in daylight. Sea dark and huge. No sun. Mustard tinge to low clouds. Humidly warm as if we're in a washing machine before the drying cycle.

All of us have cuts and scratches—from flying debris, I suppose.

Can't find first aid kit. All the seniors tried to find it, scoured the sand and the scrub behind the beach but no luck.

We've put a screen of palm fronds around Sandy's body. The sleeping bag is practically buried by sand already. It's so awful. I can't think straight. My head hurts.

I just want to be home with Mum and Dad. The worst thing is that we can't contact anyone! No phones on this island. We have to wait until the boat comes back before anyone knows what's happened to us.

Mrs Campbell says we *must* dry our sleeping bags: it's a priority. We hang them up inside out where we can on shrubs or spread them on the big rocks, weighing them down with stones, and light a fire nearby in a shallow pit. Matches and food supplies are safe in an airtight box in Mrs Campbell's kit. My poor journal is wet, but I'm trying to dry it on a rock out of the wind. Some of the pages are stuck together. But at least it's survived.

Natalie cut a leg when she fell on jagged rocks last night and is whimpering like a puppy. It looks as if it needs stitches to me, but what do I know? Worse—she's lost her blanket and her shoes. We've all been drilled by our parents to wear something on our feet all the time in case of chiggers.

'Oh that's nothing to cry about,' Mrs Campbell assures Nat. 'Don't be a baby.' She cleans the wide gash with fresh water from a water bottle and gives her a Hershey bar, which the little girl eats greedily.

Most of us went to sleep in sweatshirts and T-shirts and shorts over swimsuits. They are pretty well soaked but even without sun the air is warm and we strip off down to our swimmers and hang our wet things on a tree close to the fire.

'Right.' Mrs Campbell claps her hands. 'Now you've got your sleeping bags drying, let's see what we can find. The wind's died a little and I'm sure there'll be food, water, and most importantly, the first aid kit there somewhere.' We stand up and brush the sand from our bodies. 'Hope, you stay and look after the juniors.' Mrs Campbell waves her hand in Hope's direction, but doesn't meet her eye, so ignores Hope's look of dismay. The rest of us set off, our heads bent once again into the wind, sea spray, and sand.

We find the cases of bottled water quite easily. Buried beneath sand drifts but otherwise undamaged. There's nothing to be seen of our tents, not even on the tops of the remaining upright coconut palms; our campfire has been blown away. The banyan stands like a wooden cathedral built by a mad architect, buttresses and arches clinging to the sandy earth. Resting against one arch, as if it has been left there on purpose, is the shovel we used to dig the latrine. We pounce on it with delight. But all signs of last night's happy party have been swept clean. The tide line is littered with branches, coconuts, dead birds, dead fish, and huge hanks of seaweed like giant wide rice noodles smeared with soy sauce. Jody, who has tagged along with us, sits crying quietly on the sand, while we work our way through the debris, a dead seabird in her lap, its white neck broken. I crouch to push her hair from her eyes and plant a kiss on her head, and carry on the search.

Suddenly I see the tin barbecue, jammed between branches of a casuarina tree. Like a metal nest. Nearby we find the bag of charcoal. The brown paper wrapping has been shredded but the damp charcoal is intact. Jas and I are desperate to find the first aid bag but it seems to have vanished along with the tents. We search in the bushes and find two of the rucksacks—mine—*Thank you, God*—and May's, full of crap like make-up and face cream and hair curlers. She's ecstatic.

'Oh, May, face cream!' screeches Arlene, grabbing the jar. She takes off, dodging between fallen tree trunks, May screaming after her. 'You pig, *you pig*, bring it back. It's *mine!*'

The other rucksacks have disappeared, maybe buried or blown away. Mrs Campbell still has her nylon rucksack. She's never without it and managed to keep hold of it last night. Her guitar has gone.

'Enough, girls,' she says. 'We can come back later.'

We are blown by the fierce wind back to our rocky shelter.

'If we'd pitched camp here,' I start, but Jas holds the palm of her hand up to stop me.

'Nobody could have known,' she says. 'All we wanted to do was sit round the fire and watch the sunset.'

Thunder still rolls across the massive sea and great flashes continue all around us.

35

Once, Lan Kua told me a folk tale about how thunder and lightning came about. There's a beautiful woman who lives in the sky and has a huge glinting diamond. A giant (or is it perhaps an ogre?) covets the diamond and asks her for it but she won't give it to him. In a rage he throws his axe at her but it misses and hits the ground burying itself with a great crash. Lan Kua explained that the flashes of lightning are the shafts of light sparkling from the diamond and the thunder is the crash of the axe. I must tell the juniors this story once we're all together again.

'Look over there. Towards the mainland. What is it?' Mrs Campbell points at a billowing of thick smoke like black roses in the sky. 'Looks like an explo—'

'A lightning strike? Maybe the storm is centred over Utapao?' I interrupt her, cold at the thought of war coming to Thailand. Of course they aren't explosions. They can't be. I glance at Jas. She's looking calm as usual. No, they can't be explosions.

Those of us who are able have spent the rest of the day searching for firewood, which isn't that easy, what with the heavy rain. Jas and I put our efforts into finding kindling and trying to dry out broken off branches to put on the fire. It's a full-time job. The others are useless. May is putting her recovered curlers in her hair, Arlene is asleep or pretending to be, and Hope is holding her stomach and moaning. Jody is cuddling her bedraggled toy bear and sucking her thumb.

Carly hasn't moved. Jas says she's in shock. She wraps her in her Western Wildcats sweatshirt and gives her sips of water.

36

I'm suddenly reminded of going to see a play in Edinburgh once—Shakespeare's *The Tempest*. But then I was in the audience and now I'm centre stage and there's a real tragedy.

Mrs Campbell sits in the dark of the cave, smoking; head in her hands.

'Are you all right, Mrs Campbell?' I ask several times, and finally she answers.

'For Christ's sake, Bonnie, no I'm not all right.' She takes a bottle of Thai whisky from her backpack and drinks deeply. There's an uncomfortable silence. She's angry and I don't know what to say.

Natalie, huddled next to her, breaks the silence, howling, 'I want to go home, I want to go home.'

She sets the other juniors off and soon the three of them are sobbing their little hearts out.

We biggies try to cuddle them but Natalie won't be quieted and won't let anyone near her, and her leg is looking sore. I wish we could find the first aid kit.

'What a disaster we've lost the first aid kit!' I stare pointedly at Mrs Campbell, who ignores me. 'It could have gone in the waterproof bag with the food.'

Jas shakes her head at me, frowning. She knows how I'm feeling but she's determined to keep the peace.

The boatman will be back the day after tomorrow, and we'll have to make the best of it meanwhile. The wind is still very strong and the waves are high and we feel safer if we stay in the shelter of the rock. We've stacked a great pile of palm fronds across the cave mouth to give us more shelter from the wind.

I pull out my journal. I've started on the map on a double

page. I've named the cave *Black Cave*, because it is almost a cave and the rock is very dark with black lichens. However, I'm torn between that and *Dragon's Elbow*, which sounds more romantic and interesting. I cross out *The Landing Place* and rename it *Storm Beach*. I suddenly feel guilty. It seems inappropriate—disrespectful—to make a map when Sandy is lying dead. I replace the journal in the waterproof plastic folder with my pencil and Swiss army knife. I've attached it to my belt with a clip.

I'm still upset by Mrs Campbell's outburst. Jas comes to give me a hug, but I shake her off. I can't get over it.

Arlene and May are useless. All they talk about is boys.

'If we had boys with us they'd know what to do. Boys are good at building and stuff.'

'Yeah, Lan Kua's useful with his hands.'

'So I've heard,' May says knowingly, and Arlene smirks.

'Shut up, you two, you are so stupid!' I shout at them and they make faces at me.

I'm trying to distract myself by thinking about William Golding's book *Lord of the Flies*. Our teacher told us it was about the falling apart of society when there is no order, no authority figures. But the characters are all little boys, and everyone knows little boys are barely human. Lan Kua's little brothers are always torturing or trying to kill each other and ants, birds, snakes, dogs, their baby sister, whatever else they come across. They have to be taught that it's wrong and then they only stop because they're afraid of punishment.

They are supposed to eventually end up as peace loving Buddhists. If we're lucky.

Anyway, we're all female on this island, and *we* won't become savages.

Hope has started her period, broken her glasses, and wants to go home.

CHAPTER FOUR

14th May 74 Day 3, Morning
Didn't sleep—sleeping bag gritty and damp. My hair is
sticky and tastes of salt. My scalp is itchy with sand and
dirt. Lips are dry and cracked. Wish I'd brought lip salve
or Vaseline.

I'll never go to an island again as long as I live.

None of us feel like eating, except Hope, whose appetite
never seems to suffer no matter what happens. But Mrs
Campbell says we must.

So, just like yesterday, it's tinned sardines and cold baked
beans for brunch straight from the tin, with damp matsos.

Natalie's leg looks bad and she refuses to let Mrs
Campbell attend to it—screams if she gets close. Not that
Mrs Campbell can do much anyway without the first aid
kit. But when Natalie falls into an exhausted sleep Mrs
Campbell examines the injury. I help her clean it with bottled
water and attempt to remove dirt from the wound, which is
closing up. Mrs Campbell says it should have been stitched
and heroically sacrifices a strip of her torn petticoat-skirt to
make bandages.

'Shouldn't we clean it with hot water, Mrs Campbell? Or
disinfect it somehow?' I'm thinking of my first aid course.

'Oh, it'll be fine, Bonnie.'

Mum trained as a nurse and I'm not squeamish about blood and stuff, but the leg is red and swollen. Infections from coral cuts are common in the tropics. Some of that purple disinfectant we buy at the base shop would have been useful.

'If you fuss you'll only frighten her. We'll be home the day after tomorrow and she'll get proper medical treatment. We're doing fine for now.' This is the first time Mrs Campbell has spoken to me since her outburst last night, and I'm relieved.

I lead another search party to look for any other useful debris from last night's storm. No luck, but I do find an amazing large empty shell. I think it's a conch. I take it back with me. They had a conch in *Lord of the Flies* and used it to call the others to a meeting. And whoever spoke in meetings got to hold the conch, and all the others had to listen. I tell the others that you can blow into it and make a loud trumpeting sound, but we all try and only Hope can do it.

I suggest we tie rags over our noses and mouths to help keep the sand out. It helps.

Then Hope has a brainwave. Somehow she's managed to salvage her supply of those old-fashioned Kotex towels with loops at the end and she gives us one each to use as masks. They really work! We put the loops over our ears. We look so funny, like surgeons in a comedy movie. We laugh for the first time since our first evening on the island.

The laughter stops when we return to the cave and realize we have lost the fire. As darkness falls we huddle together, the Thai barbecue at our feet, the juniors in our arms to keep them feeling safe. Sandy's sister Carly still hasn't spoken and she's pale and listless.

'Let's sing!' Mrs Campbell smiles brightly at us.

So we sing all the songs we can think of, including Beatles and Beach Boys songs. Mrs Campbell, Arlene, and May know *all* the lyrics. We try to harmonize like the real bands do but we're rubbish.

It helps take our minds off our troubles, but I keep finding my thoughts drifting away from here.

Sandy. Could we have saved her? Her poor parents. They don't know. How will we tell them? Will Mrs Campbell tell them? Will the Thai police or USAF military police have to come to the island? We'll have to take her body back with us in the boat. My thoughts are almost noisy enough to drown out the sound of the songs and the wind and the rain.

Natalie is still asleep but it's not a natural sleep. I put my hand on her forehead like Mum does when I'm feeling ill, and she's feverish.

'What did I say about fussing?' Mrs Campbell reminds me, but not unkindly. 'You'll only upset her, or Jody . . . ' and she points at Jody, who is whispering to herself or to the invisible Mikey. But I think Natalie needs more care than we're giving her.

Mum should be here. She'd know how to help Natalie. She's the most capable person I know. Most days when she drives into Pattaya to get the groceries there's a queue of sick Thais waiting for a lift to the local clinic. Mum's become the local ambulance service, fitting in the clinic visits between shopping. One day a small child had been bitten by a pi-dog and had to have rabies injections just in case. And once our guard came out in red itchy lumps in the night and thought he had smallpox. He was very sick in the car. It turned out he had hives. He was allergic to something.

A few weeks ago a US Marine hammered at the door in the early hours of the morning. His yelling woke me. He was carrying his unconscious Thai girlfriend in his arms. She had bad head injuries. Robbers had fixed a trip wire across the road that had knocked them from his motorbike. His wallet and passport had gone.

Mum wrapped a towel around the girl's head and drove them to the all-night clinic in Pattaya. The doctor could do nothing for her and sent them by taxi to Bangkok, which is a two-hour drive away. Mum lent them the fare.

Recently the Marine returned with the cash to thank Mum for her help. His girlfriend was fine now, recovering from her injuries.

Mum always knows what's to be done. When we first arrived at Amnuythip and realized that Dad wouldn't be around much, Mum rented a car for us. There aren't any car hire firms, so she offered money to a taxi driver for the use of his car for several months. He agreed and signed the car over to her and she paid the fee. But then he kept coming to the house and demanding to have the car back. Kept saying it needed servicing, or something, but he was always drunk and Mum wouldn't let him have it. We would be stuck without it as no one else on the compound had a car except the men who have to drive to the base. Anyway, one afternoon he came to the house, drunk and sweaty, very belligerent looking, and spoke to Lek, who looked really anxious. He kept looking shiftily around, not meeting anyone's eye.

Lek translated, 'He wan' taxi now.' The squat bowlegged man paced the sandy path in front of the house.

'Tell him no, please, Lek. I have paid for six months' rental. He cannot have his car now.'

He looked very angry and Lek was shaking with fear.

'He say he nee' cab to ta' two men to Changmai.'

'Offer him tea, Lek.' Mum was smiling at him all the time, as if he was like any visitor who must be made welcome.

Mum beckoned him inside. Was she mad?

In no time he was sitting inside, reluctantly picking at biscuits and drinking tea. Mum told Lek to invite all her children for lemonade, just as if this was any old day of the week. The man mumbled angrily at Lek and she was still very nervous, biting her lip, wringing her hands and nearly in tears. Mum carried on chatting away to him in English as if he understood every word she was saying. The children sat on the polished wooden floor eating biscuits and drinking their lem-on-ay and then started jumping on the chairs and running up and down the stairs.

'Ask him if he has children, Lek, please.'

He mumbled at Lek, shamefaced.

'He say he ha' one baby, madam.'

'How lovely, how old is the baby? A boy or a girl?'

The conversation continued like that and gradually he calmed down. After about an hour Mum took his empty cup and politely showed him the door, still smiling at him. After he had staggered off Lek burst out crying. He did have a gun, she told us, and had threatened to use it.

'Why did you ask Lek to bring her children in when he was here, Mum?'

'To lighten the atmosphere, normalize things. Make him feel human, see sense. It worked.'

That night I heard a drunk staggering around in the

44

compound and I was scared the taxi driver had returned to kill us all, but Mum said it was just the guard.

I look around at us, huddling, grubby and miserable. Mum would know what to do. I'll be nicer to her when we get home.

Not that I'm horrible to her exactly, but I suppose I don't appreciate her enough. She hasn't been able to work here, (US rules for alien service wives or something) and she says it's boring, being in the middle of a war but not taking part, and wishes we'd gone back to Scotland. But then I wouldn't see anything of Daddy and that would be awful, even if he is moody when he is around. Anyway, it will be all over soon and we'll go back to our old house in Edinburgh. How lovely to wake to a big freeze and wrap up in muffler and woolly hat and walk to Holyrood Park. Perhaps we'll get a dog. I'd love a dog. Perhaps a Golden Retriever or one of those mongrels with hairy faces and intelligent eyes, the ones who look as if they can speak. In Edinburgh you see them out walking with old men, and they always look grizzled and grey—the dogs I mean.

Day 3 afternoon

I am sitting on my own in the shelter of a fallen palm to write this. The barbecue's gone out again and we've run out of charcoal. Layla Campbell is useless.

One bit of good news—Hope found Carly's teddy bear sticking out of the sand. When Hope gave it to her it was as if she didn't recognize it.

The gale isn't as bad as it was. The waves are racing in and engulfing the narrow beach. The sea is brown from churned up sand. There's a new shelf of sand where it has been moved by the storm. This sea hasn't finished with us yet.

'Mrs Campbell, don't you think it would be better if we camped on higher ground?'

'No, Bonnie, we can't leave the body . . . we can't leave it unattended.'

'But the tide is coming in and with the wind behind it, it might be even higher than last night.'

Jas supports me. 'Yes, Mrs Campbell, it doesn't feel safe here any more. The sea looks as if it will come crashing on top of us at any time.'

Mrs Campbell looks flustered for a moment. 'OK, OK, but we better bury the remains properly first and mark the grave, or we'll never find it again.'

How can she talk so coldly about Sandy?

The burial upsets us all. Mrs Campbell whispers a few words over the grave, something about Sandy being an unfortunate innocent child, but when she starts crying of course we all start. Jody wants us to chant the Amelia Earhart Cadet promise.

'OK then, why not?' says Mrs Campbell. 'How does it go?'

I am shocked. 'You must know the promise?'

'No, Bonnie, I don't know, actually. I only took the job as cadet leader because there was no one else qualified and I was persuaded to volunteer. So . . . '

'Oh.' I feel deflated.

We chant—without the benefit of Mrs Campbell's voice,

I promise to always do my best.
I promise to be honest and truthful.

46

I promise to be loyal.
I promise to be kind and thoughtful.
I promise to obey my parents.
I promise to be modest.
I promise to help my fellow cadets
whenever they need help.

We stumble through the Lord's Prayer, and sing Sandy's favourite hymn—'All Things Bright and Beautiful'. Carly and Jody make a cross pattern in shells on the mound. Mrs Campbell hasn't allowed us to make the grave very deep.

'Somebody will have to dig up her body when the boat comes,' she explains.

I look for Carly, hoping she hasn't heard.

'Now, nuts, everybody. We need to gather as many as we can—enough to keep us going until we go home.'

We set off inland, away from the roaring sea, and I try not to think of that little body, broken and alone.

There are loads of fallen coconuts all along the top of the beach, so we won't be short of something to eat and drink, except that we are in competition with coconut crabs. They're hideous and large, like shell-less hermit crabs—they split open the coconut shell with their powerful claws. They are so aggressive that we have to push them away with sticks.

Natalie can't walk, and we carry her between us, taking turns to make a seat with our arms. But she is no good at holding on as she's practically unconscious so Hope ends up carrying her over her shoulder. Luckily Natalie's small and not too heavy. Jody hangs on to Jas's arm and

47

cries incessantly. Carly drags behind Mrs Campbell. The rest of us carry sleeping bags, the remaining rucksacks, water bottles, and the waterproof bag and the rest of our food.

'Watch out for thorny bamboos and scorpions and biting ants,' Jas tells us. Mrs Campbell looks alarmed and Jas nods at her. 'Yes. And there could be snakes. What am I saying? There are bound to be snakes.' May and Arlene leap to Mrs Campbell's side, shrieking stupidly. Jas smiles cheerfully at them and rolls her eyes at me.

At least this trek will give me an opportunity to fill in more features on my map and I try to take mental photographs so that it is as accurate as possible. Dad will want to see it when I get home. We clamber over slippery rocks, helping the juniors and Hope where it's steep. There are narrow paths and climbing vines to cling to and we are now in a small jungle of palms, the high leaves clapping like wild applause in a football stadium. No birds though. I wonder if they were all blown away in the storm. Or did I imagine that cloud of birds? No one else saw it. Steam rises from the forest floor and surrounds us like a fog, and when we stop for a rest I take out my map, quickly draw three palm trees and label it *The Forest of Murk*. Or the *Maze of Mosquitoes*. I'll decide later. If I could I would think of a word beginning with J to go with jungle, but all I can think of is jade, which describes the colour of some of the trees and plants, but others are emerald or viridian.

The air is full of biting insects, and we flap at them constantly as we walk. Thank goodness Mum packed a brand new tube of insect-repellent cream. I share it with the others. It only has to last a day or so.

Suddenly we come to a halt, almost crashing into each other.

'Oh no!' Arlene has walked straight through a huge spider's web and has bits of it stuck to her hair and clothes.

'There's the spider, Spider-eyes, it's in your hair,' jokes May, and Arlene screams.

'No it isn't, don't be silly, May.' Mrs Campbell is hot and cross. We all are.

'Look out for snakes.' May has the last word as usual.

Hope keeps tripping over lianas and roots of trees. She has taken off her one-eye specs and put them away, so now she is practically blind. She's had to hand over the care of Natalie to Mrs Campbell, but because *she's* not very strong, we big ones take turns carrying the poor child.

We climb uphill for quite a while, resting every few minutes as it's hard work and our shoulders are aching like mad. Everyone has sores and cuts. I try wrapping large leaves around my ankles to protect them and it helps. Some of the others copy me. 'You're a genius,' Jas tells me, and we both wrap leaves around Hope's ankles.

All of a sudden, just as we're beginning to think we'll never stop climbing, we hear the sound of running water. It's a rushing stream, where tall canes clatter and palm fronds whisper and we top up our water bottles. There are huge moths, I think, not butterflies, enormous. Lizards dart under rocks. You know they are there but they disappear as soon as you look at them, like tiny green ghosts. Long spear-like leaves shiver and tremble.

'Look, a hornbill!' Jas points to where the top-heavy bird is sitting high up in a tree. At least one has survived then. Just then, with a whirr of wings, several hornbills appear, and

49

go to roost in the same tree. They land with a loud zipping noise. Their wings look like hands of thick fingers spread wide. They clatter and hop, screwing their strange top-heavy bills around and contorting themselves to get the right angle on a choice piece of fruit, making loud and ugly honking sounds.

Scarlet hibiscus flowers glow like lamps from the dark shade of foliage.

Jas keeps up a running commentary on what we can see. I know she's trying to keep our spirits up, but the juniors aren't interested in anything.

'Here's our fresh water supply,' Jas tells us.

'But we've enough bottles to last.' May is unimpressed.

'Let's hope so,' replies Jas, but so quietly that I think I was the only one to hear.

The wind is less noisy under the shelter of the trees, but as we finally reach the top of the hill a terrific blast hits us and we can hardly speak. We look out at the windward side of the island, where huge waves are battering the shoreline. I can't imagine anyone being brave enough to sail here to collect us if it's still this rough tomorrow.

It's a good place to view the island. I sit down and take out the map to make further drawings. There's a thick jungle over towards the west, hidden by a low mist clinging to the mountaintop. The island is almost the shape of a circle, but with a long thin tail, like a tadpole, *Dragon Point*, and has only one big beach as far as we can see, our landing beach, *Storm Beach* in the east. There are others, which make very thin white lines on the edges of the jungle. I try to draw them in the correct places.

Nobody says much for a few minutes. We're trying to catch our breath.

'We better go back to the original cave, I think,' says Mrs Campbell. 'I don't think we've seen anywhere better than that to shelter from the wind.'

May and Arlene explode in dismay.

'No, no! I can't do it!'

'You gotta be joking! We climbed all this way and you want us to go back?'

The juniors are silent, too exhausted to speak. Natalie is pale and sweating and her breath smells bad. Jas lays her down on the ground and rubs her sore arms.

'OK, OK, we'll go a little way back and sleep by the stream.' Mrs Campbell sets off back down the hill. She doesn't even offer to help us carry Natalie.

'I'll carry her, Jas.'

'Please, for a while. I'm whacked.' Her thick dark hair sticks to her forehead and scalp like a helmet.

An hour later we are lying uncomfortably in our sleeping bags on rocks or leaf litter near the stream. I don't want to risk taking my journal out here, so I try to memorize the sights and sounds. I name this place the *Gorge of Despondency*, or like A. A. Milne, I could call it *Eeyore's Gloomy Place*. I know—*The Gorge of Gloom*.

There's no overhead shelter but thankfully the rain has stopped, for now, though the trees drip on us still. We have eaten the rest of the tinned fish and beans and some dried apricots. Mrs Campbell said to chew them thoroughly before we swallow them or they'll swell up in our stomachs. Who cares? That's the least of our worries, I would have thought. Mosquitoes are tormenting us, in spite of the repellent; Hope is particularly bothered.

'Is this really the best place to camp?' I ask nobody in

particular. Jas is too busy trying to get comfortable to meet my eye and the others ignore me.

'Let's just make the best of it, shall we?' Mrs Campbell says after a few moments and I smile awkwardly at her.

Every few minutes I watch her press a damp cloth to Natalie's closed mouth. Jody sleeps. Carly still hasn't spoken. Even Jas is rather quiet tonight. She has placed her sleeping bag near to mine and is sharing it with Carly. Jody is tucked in close to Jas on the other side. Mrs Campbell is next to Jody and the other girls are further down the slope, not happy, grousing all the time about the damp and discomfort. But it's suddenly dark and I'm so exhausted I could sleep for America. Somehow my toothbrush has gone missing. I would give anything to be able to clean my teeth.

CHAPTER FiVE

The dark begins to dissolve. Another awful night. I was too uncomfortable to get much sleep, what with headache, itchy legs, and the sound of Hope slapping herself and swearing, but most of all I was worried about the 'explosions' we saw. What has been happening?

And then, as we all emerged from our sleeping bags Arlene found a leech on her leg. Mrs Campbell got it off with a lit match. All of us had to remove our clothes to see if we had any leeches. We all did. Hope had two on her tummy.

It's light enough now for me to do my journal.

Day Four—Hell Island (Might name it that)
Boat comes today, thank God. I desperately need a shower.

'You don't need to waste matches, Mrs Campbell. Look!' Jas points to an inch long bloated leech on Mrs Campbell's leg. 'They're land leeches, they don't suck as strongly as water leeches. You use your fingernail to push the end with the small oral sucker. That detaches it. Then flick the other end at the same time. See, it comes off easily.'

She never fails to amaze me, my friend Jas.

I notice a raised angry rash all over my legs. I mustn't scratch—it'll go septic—but it's difficult not to.

Mrs Campbell insists we wash our hands and faces in the stream before breakfast—dried apricots and raisins, with cold fresh water. Thank goodness it's stopped raining. Once we've eaten we set off.

I'm worried about Natalie. She has stopped moaning and is limp and pale. There were six leeches on her neck this morning, like tiny vampires. Her sister Jody is almost as pale. The other girls are fine, except Hope, who can hardly see to walk down the hill. We have to help her, telling her when there's a rock on the path or an overhanging spiky vine.

'Didn't you bring a spare pair of glasses, Hope?' Mrs Campbell asks.

'No, M-Mrs Campbell, I broke them the d-day before we c-c-came. Dad says I'm c-c-c-congenitally c-c-c-clumsy.' Hope's occasional stutter is getting worse.

'Ya, Spaz!'

'Hopeless Hope . . . '

'Don't be so cruel,' I bark.

'Ya spaz lover!'

The Barbies are so ignorant. I kick sandy soil in their direction and they run away laughing.

We head back to Storm Beach to wait for the boat. It seems like weeks ago that we landed here, not days.

The sea is enormous: I've never seen such huge waves.

We have all our belongings bundled up ready. The sleeping bags are still damp but it doesn't matter as we can wash and dry them at the Laundromat when we get home.

I glance round at us all and suddenly realize how awful we look. May and Arlene have mascara and red lipstick smudged all over their faces, and their hair looks like squashed bails of straw. Barbie dolls pulled through a hedge backwards. Hope is, well, Hope, only more so—no glasses, so her poor eyesight makes her look like a cross pink giant. (She's at least five foot ten.)

Mrs Campbell is a duchess no longer, more like what Mum would call trailer-trash. She looks exhausted, wrecked, her eyes are red-rimmed and she has frown lines between her eyes. Her hair is stuck to her head. She keeps swigging from a bottle and I know it isn't water. We're bruised and scratched and bitten to bits. May is dabbing nail varnish onto her chigger bites.

'Does that help the itching?'

'Yeah.'

'I think you should share it with the juniors,' I say.

'Do you? Well, stuff you, Bonnie MacDonald. It's mine.' Now she's putting curlers in her sticky hair again.

The juniors are all in a heap, like frightened monkeys. Natalie is totally out of it, shivering and sweaty, pallid and clammy. Occasionally she wakes and moans, her eyes disappearing up into her head. Mrs Campbell has made her as comfortable as possible wrapped in her sleeping bag.

Jas, the only one of us still looking human, stands on the fallen trunk of a palm tree, her hands shielding her eyes, watching for the boat. She looks like an heroic Amazon warrior.

They know we are expecting to leave today, so someone should come, no matter what.

Two hours later and there's no sign of a boat. Nobody has spoken for ages—our eyes have been searching the sea.

'It was this beach, wasn't it?' Mrs Campbell sounds desperate.

It's about midday. The sun, if we could only see it, is immediately overhead.

'I don't think he's coming,' sobbed Arlene.

'Shh, you'll set off the juniors.'

'W-w-we'll eat the rest of the food, that'll m-make us feel m-more cheerful,' suggests Hope.

'No, no, we better not.' Mrs Campbell is adamant.

We wait, and wait, and wait. The interminable screech of wind is driving me insane. My eyes are sore from sand. I can't even write in my journal in these conditions. Mrs Campbell walks off towards Dragon Point, at the end of the beach. Suddenly she waves her arms frantically and runs back along the shore towards us, but she's not smiling.

'Hope, stay with the juniors, you others come with me.'

'W-why is it always m-me who has to baby-sit?' Hope flops down on the sand.

We follow Mrs Campbell.

'What is it, Mrs Campbell?' Arlene asks.

'The boat—it's wrecked on the rocks. Our boat . . . '

'The boatman?' I ask, fearfully.

'I don't know. There's no sign of him.' She puts her fists to her mouth.

We scramble onto the rocks and look to where she points. The tail of the dragon, the black rocks, form a long spiky reef. The waves break over them with great intensity, and then I see it. The broken back of the hull, its ribs shattered, water pouring through the broken bones. The outboard motor is still attached to a chunk of the stern, its propeller emerging from the sea between waves.

'Oh! No!' The boat is not a boat any more, more like a dead sea bird, or a child's toy, small and smashed and dead.

'Oh my God!' shouts Arlene, sobbing in horror.

'Where is he, where is he?' May is hysterical.

'There's nothing we can do,' says Mrs Campbell.

'But can't we get to him? He might be there; he might be alive.' Jas starts to clamber along the slippery rocks out towards the wreck.

'Come back, no, it's too dangerous.' Mrs Campbell tries to stop us, but Jas and I jump from rock to rock and crouch to hang on when a large wave breaks over us, the wind tugging at our wet hair and clothes. Then there's a big gap where no rocks are showing and we can't get any further without plunging into the foam, and we aren't brave enough. We can't see the boatman. We call and call, but there's no reply. He's gone, drowned, lost.

Mrs Campbell doesn't scold us when we scramble back to the shore. She's crouched, her hands over her face, crying. May and Arlene are huddled with her. There's nothing to say. After a few moments, she rises from the sand and heads back towards the others. Hope has been standing, watching us. They know something's wrong. There's no point in hiding the truth.

'He's not coming to get us. The boat is wrecked.' Mrs Campbell half speaks the words, half sobs them. There's disbelief, silence.

'I don't understand. Why can't we go home? I want to go home now. Mikey wants to go home now.' Jody throws herself face down into the sand and sobs.

'When the storm passes someone else will come to get us,' says Jas. She and I hold each other and cry.

It must be about 2 p.m., and we've eaten nothing but salted peanuts and dried fruit all day. We trudge back to Black Cave. Our tin fire is there. No dry charcoal though.

CHAPTER SIX

Day 5
Yesterday was the worst day.

I was walking along the beach trying to remember what Lan Kua looks like. His smile. Thinking about Mum. Wishing I was home helping her with something. I never help her. I leave all that domestic stuff to Lek. And Dad—why do we rub each other up the wrong way? When did I stop being his little pussycat and become an annoying pest?

I noticed May and Arlene—those really annoying pests—sitting in the shallows together, chatting as if nothing was wrong with the world. Suddenly they leapt up, screaming, and pointing at something washing in with the waves.

I ran to see what it was. A dead dolphin or large fish? No, it was the boatman's body, or what was left of it. He didn't look human any more. It looked as if a shark had attacked him; most of one leg was gone together with a chunk from his side.

It is impossible to push the image of the body from my mind. The torn flesh was like white shreds of overcooked chicken, his one eye stared and in his empty eye-socket sat a small transparent ghost crab. His eye patch was around his neck. I don't think I'll ever forget that crab crawling out of his eye socket. May and Arlene staggered off to vomit in the sand. Acid rose in my throat and I felt faint, but after I bowed my head for a minute, the dizziness went away. Hope and Mrs Campbell had come to see what the fuss was about. Hope was the lucky one: she couldn't really see the extent of his mutilation.

'We'll need to take the eye-patch back as proof . . . for his family . . . ' Mrs Campbell signalled to Jas to pull it from the body's neck. Jas did as she was told, but I thought she'd be sick. She handed it to Mrs Campbell who pushed it into her rucksack.

'Now we must bury him. We'll need to dig a shallow grave. Bonnie, fetch the shovel. The rest of you, help pull him up the beach.'

He looked so slight and small, but no one wanted to lift his legs. In the end Hope offered to drag him on her own and Mrs Campbell just shrugged. Hope's amazingly strong. He wasn't bleeding or anything; just whitened bones and bloodless flesh. He was not like an old man—more like a skinny boy. The one-legged trail he left in the sand was faint and shallow, like a bicycle track. The drifting sand soon covered it.

Jas, Mrs Campbell, Hope, and I buried him above the water line, in a shallow pit, with stones on top of his body, like a cowboy's grave in the desert.

Jody wanted to place a cross on the grave, but Mrs Campbell pointed out that he was probably Buddhist so we just tucked a handful of tiny yellow flowers between the gravestones. Mrs Campbell said we should all pray for his soul, but I'm afraid I prayed that someone would come and rescue us soon. Jody insisted on singing 'God bless America'.

We all cried.

On our compound at Amnuythip there are two spirit houses on a raised platform, where the Thais place bowls of rice, fresh jasmine wreaths and incense every day to keep the spirits happy. Perhaps we should build one here. There are two wandering spirits now.

Day 5 afternoon
How the hell are we going to get home now? Is there a home to go back to? What were those explosions?

I worry about Sandy's body. It must be deteriorating quickly. Surely rats and other small creatures will start to eat it. I keep hearing strange noises in the night. Like an animal grunting. A wild boar? I know they live in thick forests, and we saw one here, in the centre of the island. There are still black bears, monkeys, tigers, and even wild elephants somewhere in Thailand. In the forests of the north anyway. We should have buried Sandy's body deeper.

Natalie's leg isn't any better. If anything, it's worse.

'Mrs Campbell, couldn't you use whisky as an antiseptic? Don't they do that in old Westerns? Or do they use it as an anaesthetic?'

'I don't think so.'

'But couldn't we try?'

'It's all gone, Bonnie.'

'All gone? But, there was a nearly full bottle.'

'It's gone, OK?' She won't look me in the eye.

We made a fire but couldn't find enough dry material to feed it all night and it's gone out.

'What's that?'

'It's OK, Jody, it's only a wild pig.'

'How do you know, Bonnie MacDonald? It could be a fierce baboon or something.'

'Shut up, May. Don't frighten the juniors.'

'Yeah, shut up, May,' says Arlene, who is thanked with a clout from May; she is accustomed to Arlene agreeing with her every word.

Every time the juniors open their mouths it's to beg to go home or to complain about something, and they can't understand why no one has come to fetch us. We have to watch them constantly.

We ate the last of the raisins for supper and shared a coconut amongst us for supper. Almost everything else has been eaten.

Natalie is unconscious.

I'm going to cry. No, I won't. I take out my journal. It's battered and scuffed around the edges.

This has been the worst day of my life.

I can't think of anything else to write.

CHAPTER SEVEN

Day Six

Jas has suggested I make a list of our remaining food, equipment and other supplies. I wander round what remains of the campsite, trying to make sure I don't miss anything:

Half a packet of dried apricots
Empty salted peanut tin—good for heating water?
Empty baked bean tins—for heating water?
Packet of raisins
Unlimited water—thank goodness
Salt (in case of dehydration)
4 large water bottles
A bottle of Cola
One shovel—for the latrine, and digging pits and graves
Three exercise books and two pencils
My Zen and the Art . . . book
My journal
Four flashlights and eight batteries
8 sleeping bags
Two towels
Two toilet rolls

A waterproof watch—mine
A hand mirror—May's
Scarlet lipstick—May's
Black mascara—May's
Curlers—May's
Bottle of suntan oil—May's
A comb, three hairpins, and a ponytail clip—May's
Swiss army knife—mine

It's the one Dad gave me last Christmas and I can't bear to think of it as a communal item.

A pair of broken glasses (one cracked lens, one missing)—Hope's
Two teddy bears

Sandy's was buried with her.

A kid's cuddly blanket—Natalie's
A black eye patch—in Mrs Campbell's rucksack
One plastic carrier bag
One waterproof bag
Insect bite ointment
Thai tin cooker
Two packets of Thai Safety Matches
A packet of filter cigarettes (May's)
Hand fishing line and hook
Fishing net on pole
Mrs Campbell's backpack—

'What else is in your backpack, Mrs Campbell?' I know she hasn't listed everything that's in there.

'My life support system and personal medication,' she says and walks away from me.

Wreckage from the boat has begun to appear on the beach. The waves must have lifted it from the rocks. We had already found the remains of a very long fishing line and hooks, and then a large piece of canvas still attached to the broken wooden mast, a coil of nylon rope, a torn fishing net, and best of all a curved steel knife with a cork handle. The outboard motor has been washed in too, still attached to a splintered stern-post.

More to add to the list in my journal.

More dead birds litter the tide line.

After a group discussion we decided to build a proper shelter. The Black Cave is too small for us all to fit into and I know I'm not the only one to have heard the odd grunt and squeal coming from the forest behind the beach, so it's important that we plan carefully. Before we set off to gather the building materials, I pull out my journal again.

Is Lan Kua missing me?
What is Mum doing?
Are they OK?

Day Six—Afternoon
Spent most of the morning at the top of the beach, building a
raised platform from bamboo poles lashed together with rope,
and a roof from the washed-up canvas, propped up with the
broken mast and some bamboo poles. It took ages and my arms

65

ache. It's better than nothing. Makes me feel like I'm actually doing something to help us all survive.

We have also built a fire at the top of Storm Beach, close to Black Cave on slightly higher ground where trees have been felled in the storm, as a signal to passing boats. Not that we've seen any.

The waves are still fearsome. The fire is producing a thin ribbon of smoke as the wood is damp, and we need more smoke, lots of smoke.

Jas and I decide to go on hunter-gatherer duty. We pick up the fishing gear and set off along the beach.

'Why don't you get off your fat arses and find some wood?' I shout at the Barbie Babes, who are sitting on a rock swinging their legs and doing nothing as usual.

'Go to hell, Bonnie Goodie Two Shoes MacDonald. Who do you think you are, anyway?' says May.

'Do it yourself,' sneers Arlene.

'Come on, you two, I'll help,' says Hope, who has been sitting on the sand biting her nails.

'Yes, go on, please get some more wood,' pleads Mrs Campbell, who is lying as close to the fire as she can get without setting herself alight. Reluctantly they rise and go with Hope, off into the forest. The juniors huddle together close to Mrs Campbell.

'These limpets are impossible.' Jas's face is screwed up with the effort. 'It's so frustrating. Ouch!' She shakes her hand free of the pain. 'We could eat them, if only we could get them off these rocks . . .'

Then I spot transparent shrimps darting backwards in a rock pool. We manage to get a few handfuls and carry them in the plastic bag back to the camp. We cook them very quickly in a clam shell full of seawater, at the edge of the fire.

'These are the most delicious food I have ever tasted.' I am delighted with my easy-cook meal.

'What we could do is collect more of the shrimps and use them as bait to catch something bigger and more sustaining,' says the ever sensible Jas. But I can tell she's as buoyed up by our lucky break as I am.

'Save the big shell,' I tell the others, 'they make great saucepans.' May and Arlene make a face at each other but Hope rinses out the shrimpy remains and stores the shell at the back of the shelter.

'Come on, girls.' Mrs Campbell stands and stretches. 'Who's going to help find something more to eat? And more firewood? Hope was the only one of you to come back with anything. It doesn't look as if we are going to be picked up today.' Jas and I stand up too. But the others just stare into the embers of the fire. 'For all we know there could be bananas, birds' eggs, edible roots, mangoes, and maybe other kinds of nuts. It's a tropical island, for goodness' sake, there's bound to be lots of edible stuff.' Mrs Campbell's encouragement has no effect on the other three so Jas and I set off behind her round the edge of the forest.

It's dark under the green canopy of tall trees, and we take turns to cut away thorny bamboo stalks with my Swiss army knife and the boatman's knife. It's very hard work. My hands are soon covered in blisters. There are countless terrible noises here; you wouldn't believe the uncanny sounds. A huge flying bug sounds just like a Lambretta. There's a loud honking up in the branches, but we don't

67

see what makes the racket. Then a sudden creaking, and a falling tree crashes down and just misses Jas. She's a nervous wreck, shaking with fear. I give her a hug and a smile, and Mrs Campbell suggests that we rest for a moment and drink.

'Half the problem is dehydration . . . ' she explains. But suddenly there's a loud humming from behind us and Mrs Campbell shouts, 'Get down,' and we duck as a swarm of bees passes overhead. God, I hate this place.

'Bees mean honey,' says Mrs Campbell. 'But they build their nests high up in the canopy. We'll never get to it.'

'I can climb,' I say. Gymnastics is one of my strong subjects.

'And how would you collect the honey without being stung?'

'Uh, OK, let's forget that idea.' I feel stupid and angry at the same time.

We gather up some long aromatic black bean pods.

'I don't know what they are,' says Jas, 'but they might be edible, and they'd be fuel for the fire, if nothing else.' She always talks sense. There are many newly fallen trees, uprooted in the storm. Pink orchids lie crushed under thick branches. I find a peacock feather, its golden eye shining in the gloom. The sudden beauty is so welcome.

And then we stumble upon a comb of honey, in the bole of a fallen tree. We scoop the honey from the wax cells with our fingers and eat it there and then.

'Look out for bees,' warns Mrs Campbell, but she eats just as much as Jas and I do. 'No point in trying to carry it back to the others, we'd be stung to death.'

We are cheered tremendously by the sugar rush and set off

again with high hopes of finding more good things to eat. But before long we come to an enormous gulch, completely hidden by thorny bamboo. Jas scouts round but she can't find a way through.

'We'll have to go back, the light's fading,' says Mrs Campbell. I am so disappointed. All we have to show, apart from cuts and scratches and sore legs, are bean pods, the feather, and some dry sticks and hairy lichens that will make good tinder, according to Mrs Campbell. We follow our trail back the way we came. The Barbie Babes don't even ask how we got on. Hope is scratching at her legs and has long red marks on her arms where she has scratched too hard. She looks very miserable. I wonder if the Barbie Babes have been giving her a hard time while we've been away. I wouldn't put it past them. The juniors are listless too, not playing or talking, just curled up together by the cooling fire. I get my journal out and go and sit away from the others.

Day Six continued:
I have thought of a name for the forest—Nitnoi Forest. Nitnoi means very small. The Prince of Thailand has a poodle called Nitnoi. He came to the yacht club at Pattaya once with his poodle and I met him. I quite liked the poodle.

It's good to think of another life, away from this dreadful island, this prison.

While we've been gone Hope has somehow dragged the outboard motor up the beach by herself and placed it close to the fire: to dry it out, she explains.

'You don't think we could get it to work, do you?' I ask her and she shrugs.

'M-m-maybe, who knows?' She looks disappointed at my lack of enthusiasm.

'Hope, are you OK?'

'Yeah, I'm OK.'

'Are those stupid girls being horrible to you?'

'M-m-may and Arl-l-l-lene? No, no m-m-more than usual.' She tries to smile.

'You must stand up to them,' I say. I mean to sound sympathetic, but it sounds like an accusation. Jas does these things so much better than me.

The fire is useless as a signal—no flames, only a thin wispy smoke trail which is immediately dispersed by the strong wind. Hope points to the juniors. They're making their way back along the beach, their arms full of coconut husks, and more importantly, coconuts. I still can't summon up the energy to respond as brightly as I know Hope wishes I would, but Mrs Campbell saves the moment.

'That's great, girls,' she calls to them. 'With coconuts we won't go hungry or thirsty.' And she sets about opening one of the shells, hitting it with the boatman's blade. Eventually it cracks open and we all have a sip of the milk, a thin white liquid that tastes sweet and refreshing. The flesh is half set, a jelly-like substance like yoghurt, rather disgusting, but we eat it ravenously. What I wouldn't do for a glass of iced star-fruit juice.

I re-open out my journal.

If we ever leave here I am never going to eat another coconut as long as I live.

And then tuck it away.

Mrs Campbell opens another coconut shell and takes it to give to Natalie. She is back in a moment.

'Where's Natalie?'

'We put her over there, we couldn't stand the smell.' Arlene shrugs her pink shoulders and makes a face. She points to a blue sleeping bag further along the top of the beach.

'You did what?' Mrs Campbell runs to where they've left the little girl, under the wispy shade of the casuarina trees. I follow. The smell is pretty unbearable. She's leaning over the child, holding her head up to take the liquid. Natalie splutters and the milk trickles out of the side of her mouth. She looks awful, flushed and dry-mouthed. Mrs Campbell presses more milk to her lips and this time she takes a little.

'I'll have to change her dressing.'

'I'll help, Mrs Campbell. Shall I heat some water?'

'What will you heat it in?'

'Coconut shells? They'll hold more than Jas's clam shell.'

'Good idea, Bonnie, brilliant!' One moment she's being horrid and the next she's trying to be nice.

I stand the shells jammed between rocks over the embers of the fire and the water soon warms up. The difficult thing is carrying the hot shells up to the patient. In the end I use my T-shirt as an oven mitt and push the shell into the sand near Natalie.

'Don't you think the stream must come out on the beach somewhere, Mrs Campbell? We can't climb to the Gorge of Gloom all the time for water.'

'Oh, Bonnie, stop nagging,' Mrs Campbell shouts at me, and I cringe at her sudden change of mood. She carries on tending to the sick child, and I hide my red face under my hair.

Mrs Campbell tests the warm water with her elbow, like seeing if the bath is too hot for a baby, and it is, and her jerking arm knocks the coconut shell over and all the water spills onto the sand.

I start again from scratch, but don't leave it to heat for so long. This time it is the right temperature and Mrs Campbell bathes Natalie's leg. She hardly makes a sound.

'Why does it smell so bad, Mrs Campbell?'

'It's the infection, Bonnie, it's not looking good. I think it's gangrene.'

The leg is swollen all the way up.

I hold my nose. I can't help it.

'You don't have to stay. I can manage now.'

'OK, if you're sure.'

The sun has come out at last and the bigger girls are swimming in the fishing pool, the juniors splashing in the shallows. I run back to the edge of the sea and stare out at the laughing girls. There's a huge black cloud on the horizon.

I look back and see Mrs Campbell sitting smoking, six feet of sand between her and Natalie.

CHAPTER EiGHT

Day 7
*Cried myself to sleep last night. Mrs Campbell's useless as a
cadet leader, useless as a carer, useless as a friend. I hate her.*

Rain all night, and we didn't get much sleep, what with
the hooting of the gibbons and unidentified screams and
coughs.

This morning the rain's stopped and the wind has
dropped, thank goodness. Little spots of silver dance on
the sea and it almost makes me forget the awfulness of the
past few days, though I'm worn out from crying.

'You OK, Bonz?' Jas looks worriedly at me. 'You don't
look so good this morning.'

'Think you're a better sight, do you?' I snap. Don't know
what's the matter with me. I never speak cruelly to Jas. She
wanders off to wash. I ought to run after her. Apologize.
But I'm too tired and sore and miserable. I sit on a tall rock
at the water's edge. On my own.

The lagoon has all the colours of a peacock's feather.
Pink coral heads are visible, and red and purple weed swirls,
lifts, and falls on the gentle waves. The palms' feathery
heads quiver in the breeze and huge butterflies flutter on
the suddenly brilliant flowers at the top of the beach. It is

paradise, I tell myself. Or it would be if it weren't for the dead birds rotting on the tide line, hundreds of them. Fat flies swarm over the broken gulls, parakeets, bush turkeys, even peacocks. I catch sight of a rat moving among the carcasses. That'll freak out the Barbie Babes.

Hope and Jas come down the beach armed with plastic bags.

'We can't let anyone swim until we've cleared them,' Jas calls over to me, a kind of 'Can we be friends again?' tone to her voice, and I'm glad. I swing down from my rock and make enough of a commotion to send the marauding rats back to where they came from.

Hope, Jas, and I spend the whole morning gathering the corpses in a stinking heap, intending to bury them at the other end of the beach, but it's a disgusting job. We bind the plastic bags round our hands and wrap T-shirts over our mouths and noses.

Once the beach is mostly clear of rotting creatures, Carly and Jody are paddling. They have taken off all their clothes and seem happy enough, though Carly still hasn't spoken as far as I know. Hope and I are washing their things in a fresh water spring that Jas and I found on the way back from the burial site. It was only a matter of searching along the top of the beach. It bubbles up by rocks just inside the bordering trees, and then disappears again under the sand.

'It's a happy coincidence that the stream is well away from the latrine,' I told Mrs Campbell, but she didn't respond.

Hope looks vulnerable without her specs. Like a blind owl.

74

'Do you think w-we are going to get r-r-r-r-rescued, Bonnie?'

'Yeah, sure we are, Hope. Now the wind has dropped they'll send a boat.'

Hope doesn't look convinced.

'I wish I hadn't b-broken m-my specs. I can't see a thing. It's like living in a thick m-mist.'

'Have you always worn them?'

'Since I was very little. M-m-mum says she's going to get m-me contact lenses soon. And she's going to get m-my t-t-t-t-teeth fixed. But Dad says why b-b-b-b-bother? It w-w-w-w-won't make me look any m-m-m-more human. Is this shirt clean enough, do you think?'

We hang the clothes across a fallen palm trunk and turn when we hear happy shrieking.

I can't believe my eyes. May, Arlene, and Mrs Campbell are skinny-dipping in the fishing pool. They've done nothing to help all morning. And then I realize there's no fire. They've allowed it to go out. They come up the beach, naked. I'm embarrassed but also very angry.

'Mrs Campbell, shouldn't we keep the fire burning as a marker for anyone coming to rescue us?'

She throws herself down on the sand, ignoring me once again. I march over to her and stand, my hands on my hips, looking down at her.

'Shut up, Bonnie MacDonald. You're so bossy,' says May, stretching out close to Mrs Campbell.

'Oh, they'll find us now the weather's improved,' Mrs Campbell mumbles and rolls a cigarette. I can't remember ever feeling this angry before: she's wasting matches now.

'Your cigarette smells funny, Mrs Campbell.'

'Herbal,' she says, sucking in deeply.

Oh yeah, right, herbal. Pull the other one. I don't trust myself to speak and walk away. Jas looks at me, her eyes asking me what's happened but I shake my head, dropping cross-legged onto the sand, my head in my hands.

The day crawls on. No one comes. We don't see any boats, or planes or helicopters. When I suggest a hunt for more provisions only Jas says yes. No one else wants to come. All the others do is swim and muck about. It's as if they are on holiday. It's as if Sandy hasn't died, or the boatman. As if Natalie isn't seriously sick. As if we aren't stuck here until someone finds us.

Hope mopes on her own, the only girl with all her clothes on, though she looks far too hot.

'Coming?' I ask but she shakes her head.

'Then keep an eye on Natalie, will you?'

Hope nods and moves closer to where Natalie is lying.

'It's one thing the juniors acting as if nothing's happened, but you'd expect Mrs Campbell and the others to act responsibly,' I grumble.

'In denial,' says Jas. 'All in denial.' (Her mother's a psychologist.)

'But think about it, Jas. Who knows we're here? No one. If the boatman had got home it would be different, but there are hundreds, well, dozens of islands. How will they know where to find us?'

'We haven't seen any boats or planes today.' For once Jas can't look on the bright side. 'Why? Why aren't they even looking for us? Something awful must have happened at the base.'

We look at each other. Has there been an air strike?

Or was the storm so bad the base was flooded or destroyed?

'What's that tree? Is it a mango?'

'Yes, look, fresh fruit!'

We gather the fallen fruit, braving the wasps and flies, and eat. Sweetness explodes in my mouth. I suddenly start crying, I don't know why. Jas puts her arm around me and we sob together.

I've found out why Mrs Campbell has given up any pretence at being responsible. For a start she had *two* bottles of whisky with her, not one, and she's nearly finished the second one. I add this information to the list in my journal. I don't know what made me look in her rucksack. Well, that's not true. I was suspicious because she's been acting so strangely—staggering around and laughing too much and then skinny-dipping with the Barbie Babes as if she's one of us instead of an adult who is supposed to be caring for us. It's not right. Not natural. There's something wrapped in silver foil—marijuana, I think.

I have poured most of the remains of the whisky into the peanut tin and hidden it near Natalie's sleeping bag. I've diluted the rest with water. I should have peed in it.

'Why don't we send a message in a bottle?' Jas knows that I need to keep busy.

'Brilliant, Jas. Why didn't we think of it before?'

The sea's still running like a tap—a bottle might be thrown on to the beach at home in a matter of hours.

On a page from my journal I draw a map of the island and show the other islands we floated past, including Ko

Chang, the inhabited one, and the mainland, and I write a short message:

SOS. HELP. MAROONED ON THIS ISLAND. 1 DEAD 8 SURVIVORS. BOATMAN DEAD.

I add our names, the dead and the survivors.

Jas, Hope, and I sign it, roll it up in a plastic bag and push it into an empty Mekong bottle. Hope thumps the stopper in with the palm of her hand, and as the tide is still on the ebb she throws it as far as she can out to sea from Dragon Point.

CHAPTER NINE

Day 8 I think.
I am confused about what day it is. We seem to have been here for ever.

I want to be on my own. I have become simply part of a doomed tribe on a desert island, trying to survive. I'm frightened. What am I frightened of? Of what am I frightened that should be. Death, of course. Though I don't think I will die, not just yet anyway. I'm fit and strong and we can't die of thirst on an island with fresh water. I might lose a bit of weight, that's all. Be more of a skinny malinkum (don't know how to spell that but it's what Dad calls me) than I am already. I am more scared of the fact that Mrs Campbell has given up looking after us. Given up being responsible.

In Zen and the Art of Motorcycle Maintenance Phaedrus says, 'The act of writing sorts out the problem.' I'll carry on writing though I can't see how it's going to help. But writing and reading give me a sense of normality, help to keep me sane. And this journal may be the only way our parents find out what happened.

Mrs Campbell has let us down badly. I used to think she was wonderful—because she seemed to understand me. But she lied to us about the whisky, when it might have helped Natalie. She's a liar and a cheat. She tricked us all. I despise her.

I've decided to name this island Koh Tabu. It's the name the boatman shouted before he set off home again. It means Forbidden Island, I think.

Jas and I are looking after Natalie now. When I offer to change the old dressings Mrs Campbell looks really relieved.

'Nurse Bonnie,' she says, but her smile isn't kindly. 'Yes, you'll make an excellent Chief Nurse.'

The little girl is unconscious. She looks grey. I try to remember details from my first aid badge which might help her. I have taken off her stained bandage—strips of Mrs Campbell's skirt—and poured some of the hidden whisky over the injured leg, which is almost black. I've wetted my T-shirt and placed it on her forehead and other pulse points in an attempt to cool her. She was far too hot so we took her out of the sleeping bag and moved her so she is in total shade. She's so weak that she can't even hold her cuddly blanket.

I sit with her for a while and fan her with a large leaf, but I can't take the stench for very long. I don't know whether to cover the injury or leave it open to the air. The first aid course didn't cover gangrene. In the end I use strips of towelling as a bandage, just to help keep the smell in and the flies away. I hate flies.

'Jas, take over for a while, will you?'

'OK. How is she?'

'Not good. We should take turns to keep her cool and give her water.'

'Sure. You better sort it. Mrs Campbell has gone to sleep.'

The juniors look hot and bothered, and have caught the sun.

'Where are your hats?' On our first day after the hurricane Jas wove us palm leaf hats. They are a bit scratchy, but they work, when they stay on.

'Who do you think you are, Bonnie MacDonald? You're not in charge.'

'We are all going to be sick or dead by the time we're rescued, if we don't act sensibly. Don't you understand? Heatstroke is not funny.' The juniors look dehydrated. 'Get some salt and water into them, straight away. And we need a rota to look after Natalie.' Someone's got to be in charge.

The Barbie Babes look daggers at me. 'If Layla didn't tell us, we don't have to do it.'

'Layla? Don't you mean Mrs Campbell?'

'She said to call her Layla. Do it yourself, bossy boots.' They flounce off together up the beach, May with her hair still in curlers.

'I'll help,' says Hope.

She takes the juniors into the shade at the top of the beach and pours salt into the palms of their hands.

'Now lick it all up and then drink lots of water,' I hear her tell them, not unkindly. They are red-faced and tearful. They lie down under the trees, whimpering and restless.

I search the far end of the beach for coconut husks and dry twigs and relight our fire. The matches are damp and I waste several trying to get a light. I lay them out on a fallen tree to dry. There aren't many left and they are the Thai matches, they bend and split if you put pressure on them.

Mrs Campbell has woken and staggers after May and Arlene.

I wander back to the edge of the sea, stand on a rock and look down into the still water of a small tidal rock pool. My vision blurred by tears. These are not tears of grief or sorrow, or of longing for home and my parents. They are tears of anger, a deep dark rage that frightens me, terrifies me. This isn't me, this furious girl staring back at me from the surface of the water. My features tremble, alter, I do not recognize myself: the grim mouth and hard eyes—a stranger.

Hope has dug a shallow trench around our campsite to take rain water away down the beach. I should have thought of that. But she doesn't stop there.

'I'm going to split some b-bamboos and make a m-more waterp-p-proof roof.'

I help her carry large bamboo poles onto the beach and watch as she splits them lengthways with my penknife. Then we carry them to the camp. Hope pushes six tall poles into the sand to make three corner supports. For the roofing she arranges the split bamboo across several straight branches, overlaid alternately to interlock with one another to make it waterproof. It looks very practical. I'm impressed.

All this takes until the early evening and after we've eaten we're all tired and subdued, and go to our sleeping bags early. I read by the light of my torch, trying to lift my mind away from our troubles. I can't think about our predicament all the time, it's too upsetting. But I can't block out the sounds of the other girls crying on their own. We're all on our own really, thinking about our homes and parents and wondering why they haven't come looking for us.

* * *

There was no rain in the night so Hope's roofing material wasn't tested. There were more weird noises—moaning and wheezing and crashing, and Jas and I clung to each other, silent and terrified. Luckily the juniors slept through it. I'm exhausted, I've never felt more tired. The sky is overcast: purple and yellow like an old bruise. I hate this place. I hate everything about it—the damp, the sand in our sleeping bags, the jungle, the insects, the sea, the sky.

There's nothing to eat except coconut but we have water. I try to gather enough energy to go back to where we found the mangoes, but I can't lift myself. Jas is still dozing.

Dad once told me you can live for ages with only clean water. He would be all right here. He had loads of survival training exercises when he joined the SAS. I remember asking him about things he ate when he was dropped from a helicopter into a jungle somewhere. He said they had nothing with them—no emergency rations or anything. They were dropped two at a time and told to find their way to the coast as fast as possible. They had no compass, no water, no matches, no sleeping bags. None of the luxuries that we have—fresh water on tap practically, sleeping bags, coconuts all over the beach, fishing gear. He and the other soldier dug up roots with their bare hands, and tried different leaves and fruit.

He told me about an edibility test you have to follow if you don't recognize a plant and I suddenly remember that I wrote it up in my journal, inside the back cover. I suppose I was trying to prove to him that I listen to what he says. I dive into my sleeping bag and pull the notebook out as if I've discovered some priceless treasure. I'm grinning like a mad person. The others look almost irritated by my sudden burst of activity, so I head over to where Natalie's lying, and read the list to her, as if it's a bedtime story. I'm glad I have the list. If I die the survivors can follow the instructions:

Edibility Test

1. Always choose young shoots or leaves, not old or withered plants.
2. Crush and smell the plant/leaf. If it smells of peaches or bitter almonds discard it.
3. If it's a strange fruit or unidentifiable root, squeeze juice or rub gently on tender skin—like your armpit. If it brings you out in a rash or itches, don't eat it.
4. If there's no irritation you can go to the next stage, which is to place a small bit on your lips. Wait a few seconds to see if there is any reaction.
5. If not, try a little in the corner of your mouth.
6. Then on the tip of the tongue.
7. Then under the tongue.
8. Chew a small portion. If you don't get sore throat, irritation, stinging or burning, swallow some.
9. Wait five hours without eating anything else and if you aren't sick or dying it's edible.

The experiment should be tried by only one person.

Natalie's face is calm, and I wonder if she can hear what I'm telling her.

'I seem to remember he said roots always have to be cooked.'

Her expression doesn't alter.

'You wouldn't eat a raw potato, would you?'

84

Still nothing, but I'm sure she's listening to me.

'I should have paid more attention,' I tell her. 'He always wanted me to listen to him, but I always wanted to get on and do things. It drives him crazy.'

I return to the list.

Plants to be avoided:

1. *Any plant with a milky sap (except dandelion).*
2. *Red plants.*
3. *Avoid fruit with tiny barbs on stems and leaves as they will irritate the mouth and digestive tract.*
4. *Avoid old withered leaves. Some develop deadly toxins when they wilt.*
5. *Avoid mature bracken.*

'Haven't seen any here anyhow,' I reassure Natalie.

6. *Only eat fungi if you can positively identify it.*

After I've finished, I suddenly remember a story Dad told me. He and his men were desperate for meat, so when they found a wild boar trail they followed it and ended up being hunted themselves. They had to climb into trees to escape. Dad said that the wild boar were very canny and attacked from the rear. Apparently, the tuskers gore you to the ground and eat you alive. I shudder and decide that it's a story Natalie doesn't need to hear.

I can't get her to take any water. I squeeze a moist cloth onto her chapped lips but she just lies there, water trickling from her mouth onto her throat and to the back of her neck. I can't look at her leg any more. Should we try to amputate it? We have a knife, two. No anaesthetic apart from whisky, though, and no clean rags to bandage the stump. The remaining towels are too dirty. The bugs might kill her. I suppose I could wash our T-shirts in boiling water and use them. It might save her life.

I can't believe I'm having to think like this. What would Mum do? I wish she were here.

Why doesn't someone come?

The wind has died. I walk down towards the shore. A load of small jellyfish have washed up on the beach. It's a battalion of Portuguese man-o'-war, men-o'-war I suppose they should be called, and their sting can be very painful if not fatal. Their deflated balloon bodies float in the swimming pool. Trailing purple tentacles are wrapped and trapped around rocks like badly tied parcels, drying in the sun, stranded by the falling tide. I sit on a rock and study one of these totally alien creatures, which is moving constantly, like a bulbous transparent nose sniffing for food. There's a neon blue-green puckered line along the edge of each balloon, like a scar.

No one may swim now—not in the pool and not in the sea. No paddling either.

Jas joins me on my rock. 'We've been invaded,' she says, and I nod.

'They aren't actually jellyfish,' she begins to explain, as we sit mesmerized by the gentle motion of the weird things, but suddenly—

'Plane, a plane! *Jas!* They're looking for us!'

'Fire, we must have fire—'

'Matches! Where are the matches?' We run up the beach, yelling.

But Mrs Campbell has the matches and she's not here. We wave our arms, take off our T-shirts and flap them like mad birds, screaming into the sky, but the plane is heading away. In a matter of seconds it's gone. At first we just stare at where it was in the sky, and then Jas and I throw ourselves onto the sand and sob in frustration. A few minutes later the others come dawdling back along the beach with Mrs Campbell, who wears a hibiscus blossom in her hair and has a cigarette hanging from her lips.

'Where the hell were you? There's *no* signal fire and *you've* got the matches.' I hurl the words at her as if they are rocks. I wish they were.

'Miss Goody Two Shoes!' She throws the matches at me. The packet is nearly empty. The matchbook has a logo with a naked girl on it advertising Tallulah Bar, Pattaya, one of the seedier hangouts in town where bar girls strip.

An odd memory suddenly hits me from about a year ago.

I'm alone with Mum in the car. We've been shopping in Pattaya for school shoes and we stop at a junction. While we wait to turn right, I see a car I recognize leaving the car park of Tallulah Bar. I remember Mum tutting at the flashing neon sign of a life-size naked dancing girl. But my eyes are staying with the car. The woman in the front passenger seat has her hair tied in a knot on her neck, and an amazing wide smile. She's smoking, and tucking a stray strand of dark red curly hair behind her ear. Jas's father, the driver, is looking at her and talking animatedly. She leans into him then bends her head to his shoulder.

'Who's that with Jas's dad, Mum?'

'Where?'

'Redhead.' Their car, a black Mercedes, has turned the corner away from us.

'Didn't see,' she said. I'm not sure she's telling the truth.

Of course it could have been totally innocent. The colonel was simply giving her a lift. But I don't think so. They looked so . . . intimate.

I glare at Mrs Campbell. I feel even more furious. My best friend Jas's father! Her mum is so pretty, or was until she had the baby and the migraines.

I look quickly at Jas. I am not going to tell her of my suspicions. She would die.

'Don't you want to be rescued?' I snarl. 'Don't you care if we don't get home?'

She sighs, as if I'm hardly worth talking to. 'To be honest, Bonnie, no, I don't care. And anyway, I think you'll find that maybe there's no *home* to go back to.'

'What do you mean?'

'Well, just what do you think was going on when the explosions happened?'

'But . . . but even if there was an attack, which there couldn't have been, we've seen aircraft looking for us, and if there's no smoke we have no chance of being spotted.'

'How do we know they are friendly aircraft?'

I am stunned into silence.

Jas says, 'Of course they're ours. No one could overcome our military just like that. That's crazy!'

'Well, light your stupid fire if you want. I don't care either way.'

'That's not good enough. We need a rota to make sure there are two fire-keepers at all times.' Jas is very strong and supportive at times like this, and the others turn to her too.

'Yes, Layla, we want a fire even if no one rescues us, otherwise we'll have to eat raw fish,' the Barbie Babes plead with her.

'OK OK. Point taken. We'll light a fire. May—you and Arlene look after the fire tonight, I'll take over at midnight.'

'Jas and I will do the dawn watch,' I say. 'And Hope can look after it during the day. The juniors can help gather wood whenever they can. We'll need all we can get. And they can't swim—the place is infested with poisonous jellyfish.'

I take some grim pleasure in their squeals of horror as I turn on my heel and walk away.

Apart from Jas I talk to nobody for the rest of the afternoon.

There's a section of beach near the rocks of Dragon Point where the sand is damp enough to build sandcastles and Jody and Carly have made a really high castle with a moat. They've decorated it with shells and coloured weed. Each day, after the tide has eaten away at its foundations, they rebuild it, rearranging the decorations and replacing faded flowers. Like the banyan, that part of the beach is theirs and we older ones don't use it. They have also built a simple seesaw using a washed up old plank of wood that's covered in goose barnacles, balanced on a large palm trunk. I watch them doing handstands and cartwheels, childish activities to block out the awful things they should never have had to witness.

Hope is crouched nearby squinting at little ghost crabs running in and out of their tunnel homes, shifting sand and making new holes. They have a complete underground system of tunnels. When one gets frightened away from his own hole he panics and tries to get into another hole, whereupon he's chased out by the real occupant. I like watching them too, but the sand flies bite if you sit in one place too long. Hope is so badly bitten now she hardly seems to notice.

Everyone is subdued this evening, after the row about the fire. I've had a gruesome thought. I can't even bring myself to share it with Jas. What if we dig up Sandy's body and use her red sleeping bag as a flag—it would be very visible from the sky. Or we could use Mrs Campbell's red petticoat. Much better. She doesn't wear it much any more anyway. The wind was tearing it and making it difficult for her to walk, tangling it in her legs. Instead she wears only her torn blouse and bikini pants. Her fair skin is sunburnt and spoiled by bruises and scratches.

Jas shuffles closer to me as we sit watching the flames.

'I don't care what she says,' she whispers to me, 'at least we know *someone* is looking for us, and something has been decided about getting off this island.'

Later in the night I wake with a strange smell in my nose. Not Natalie. On the beach, close to the fire, Mrs Campbell is sitting cross-legged with May and Arlene either side of her. I watch as the faint glow from the embers lights up their mascara and lipstick smeared faces, and I see the flare of a thick cigarette pass from one mouth to another, and then another. Loopy Layla is smiling broadly and tucking her hair behind her ears and the Barbie Babes are giggling. I feel outraged. So angry I want to be sick.

I nudge Jas awake so she can be witness to the scene too.

'What's up?'

'Look at them.'

'What are they doing?'

'What does it look like?'

'Smoking pot?'

'I reckon.'

'I don't believe it.'

'*She's* unbelievable.'

I wonder if she could be right about the base. Has it been destroyed? Are my parents safe? Have we really no homes to go back to? I take out my journal.

Why are our problems always so much worse at night? Mrs Campbell and the Barbie Babes are smoking pot.

CHAPTER TEN

Koh Tabu, Day 9
Hungry all the time.
Think Natalie's dying.
I hate LC.
Why didn't Mum come with us?

Natalie doesn't whimper or anything. Jas and I have stopped trying to do anything about her leg. We just sit with her when we can, telling her stories, hoping she can hear. Perhaps we should try to amputate. If she's going to die anyway, it wouldn't hurt to try, would it? Except she might die in excruciating pain. I feel guilty all the time.

We have a good supply of coconuts and some mangoes but it's not enough to cure the hunger pangs. My stomach makes the most awful noises. We can't catch shrimp with the man-o'-war invasion of our fishing pool. What I wouldn't give for a half-pound cheeseburger with fries. I thought Mrs Campbell was supposed to be a survival expert. She hasn't even bothered to look at Natalie's leg for two days.

The juniors are listless. They were playing skipping games with a long piece of liana as rope, but now they've no energy and they are sitting in the banyan tree, swinging their legs, staring out to sea. Clouds race across the sky and the wind is very strong again. There's an orange tinge to everything including the waves, except where they break on the reef. There they fragment into tall sprays of peach and luminous green.

Mrs Campbell, May, and Arlene Spider-eyes have ganged up together and all they do is smoke, do each other's hair and lie around half naked, giggling and stupid. When we're not sitting with Nat, Jas, Hope, and I spend all our time gathering firewood and looking for food. Hope is good at reaching figs on high branches and dragging heavy logs to the beach.

We spotted a helicopter yesterday but it came nowhere near our island. It was a very long way away. There are so many little islands and they all look alike, densely wooded like small mountains in the sea. There must be at least thirty between us and the one we were supposed to camp on.

'If they k-keep on looking they are sure to f-f-find us eventually, aren't they?' said Hope. 'M-maybe we should be more pro-active about g-getting help,' she added.

'How do you mean?' I ask.

'B-build a r-raft or something.'

'How on earth can we do that? Anyway it's too rough, it would sink and we'd drown.'

'We built a c-camp. We could use the same m-materials for a raft.'

'It wouldn't float.'

'Light m-more fires, all along the b-beach?'

'We can barely keep one fire going let alone more. No, that's stupid.'

'W-w-well, w-what do you suggest then?'

'I don't know. Write SOS in the sand.'

'The sand gets c-covered every high tide.'

'We've got no other means of signalling.'

'OK. We'll g-get the juniors to help c-collect as m-many stones and big shells as they can. We've already got quite a f-few.'

Hope has a point and it would give them something to do, help take their minds off Sandy's death and Natalie's leg. That's the idea, anyway. We work the beach, heads down looking for rocks and shells.

There's a scream.

The red sleeping bag has been dragged from its original burial place and torn apart. Sandy's body has gone. Carly has Sandy's bloody teddy bear in her arms.

I pick her up and run to Mrs Campbell.

'Mrs Campbell. Sandy's body—it's gone.'

Her eyes roll in her head, not focusing on anything. May giggles.

'Shut up, you stupid cow, *shut up*! Don't you realize the danger we're in?' I'm shouting. 'We're trapped on this island with something dangerous. Wild boar maybe, or a big cat, and you're, you're . . . '

I put Carly down and she runs off to Jody and carries on looking for shells as if nothing has happened. But something has changed. Not only are we not being rescued, we're sharing an island with an animal that eats human flesh. Probably more than one. There's no point in wasting any more time on Mrs Campbell.

We need weapons: I should have thought of it before. We'll make spears. Jas and I find more bamboo stalks of the right length and thickness. I make several spears, whittling their tips to make sharp points with my penknife. Then I have a brilliant idea—I split the end of a long cane, position the Swiss Army knife in it, open to a vicious serrated blade, and tie it on with some fishing line. On the beach I throw it as far as I can. It flies in an arc and lands blade down in the sand. It works!

But that only works for one spear and we need more. I'm desperate to keep going, keep busy. We should have one each at least. And if my army knife is stuck on the end of a pole I can't use any of its many useful blades and implements.

I find one of the baked bean tins, flatten it with a stone and then bend and cut it into a sharp cone shape, which I flatten. I fit it into the split end of the spear and bind it onto the shaft with a piece of fishing line. It looks good. I throw it several times aiming at a fallen tree trunk. It works. I craft two more spear-heads with the tins. One for Hope, one for Jas, and one for me.

'We have to keep the fire going,' I tell everybody, 'and all sleep close by.' For once nobody complains that I'm being too bossy. We've moved Natalie back to our camp and know that, in spite of the stench, we have to have her close to us at night.

Mrs Campbell seems to have sobered up. Or at least she's not as spaced out as she was. I despair of May and Arlene, who have spent all day asleep in the sun. I don't care, let them fry. They don't deserve to be looked after.

But then I discover that the matches are finished. That explains why Mrs Campbell's able to sit up and speak. Now surely she has to pay attention.

CHAPTER ELEVEN

DAY 10

I keep thinking it can't get any worse, and then it does. The nightmare is never-ending.

A fearful night. Wild boar attack in the night.

Camp destroyed.

We were woken by loud squeals and snuffling and then the barrier was down and at least three smelly creatures rampaged through the camp, even trampling the fire. It was chaos—all of us screaming and running around like headless chickens. The platform was smashed and the walls and roof collapsed. Couldn't find the spears. No one was hurt, except for Hope, who went over on her ankle. We huddled together in the darkness for the rest of the night, one torch on at all times.

Then, to cap it all, it rained hard. The fire had no chance. If we'd kept the barbecue going there would be charcoal embers we could use. I could have wrapped the glowing ember in banana leaves and carried them with me to the top of the island and made a fire. I could have carried the hot parcel in a coconut shell. We could have banana fritters, grilled fish . . .

I'm hungry and so cold.

Another day in Paradise. Must turn off the torch now to save batteries. Jas and I are on watch, though I don't think anyone can sleep.

'Bonnie, listen!' Jas is leaning over Natalie.

'What is it?'

'Do you think her breathing's changed?'

'She's too hot. I'll cool her pulse points.'

'No, Bonnie, it's too late, I think she's . . . '

I press my fingers to her throat to feel for a pulse. It's very faint.

'I don't think she's in pain,' I say.

We sit and hold her hands, warm sticky hands, still as stones. She fades away quietly, without a murmur, her skin turning grey and pallid as dawn breaks. She doesn't look like Natalie any more. I hear Jas's quiet crying in the gloom.

I feel nothing, no feeling at all. All we can do is wait for morning.

Dawn announces itself with a pea soup sky and a purple heaving sea. Large black birds circle.

Mrs Campbell became hysterical when we told her about Natalie. I really think she's gone totally out of her mind. She wailed like a baby and took off up the beach.

Jody is inconsolable. Hope tries to cuddle her, but she runs away and sits on a rock, her head on her knees.

Before the day gathers heat we bury Natalie's body as deep as we can, the remains of her cuddly blanket wrapped round her, placing rocks on top of the mound. No matter how much I wash my hands I can still smell the putrefaction.

Now we have three wandering spirits.

Jas, Hope, and I build a small shrine on a shelf at the back of Black Cave. Jas has made a sort of wreath from leaves, and I have filled a tin can with orchids.

'We have to put food out to mollify the spirits.'

'OK. A coconut.'

Shame we haven't any jasmine. Lan Kua once told me that jasmine symbolizes the beauty of the Buddha's teachings and, as it perishes, the impermanence of life.

Hope has washed Sandy's teddy bear in fresh water to get the stink and bloodstains out. Carly whispers in its ear, kisses it and places it on the shelf with the other treasures—the peacock feather, the conch, and a little pile of cowrie shells.

'I think w-w-w-we ought to have a c-c-crucifix,' says Hope.

She takes off her own silver cross and chain and places it on the rock. Jas is trying to soothe Jody, but the poor kid is exhausted with loud grief and just sits by the grave and keens.

'I'm sick of funerals. I want to live,' I say. I feel like something is strangling my heart.

Jas goes back to Jody and tries to cuddle her, but Jody pushes her away, too.

After the funeral I sit and write in my journal:

Natalie is dead.
I don't know where Mrs Campbell is and I don't care.

* * *

We—Jas and I, Hope, the Barbie Babes, Jody and Carly—
have removed our sleeping bags from the smashed platform
back to Black Cave. Mrs Campbell isn't back yet.

'Do you think we should go and look for her?' asks Jas.

'Don't care if I never see her again,' I say. And I mean
it.

Mattresses of leaves and branches help keep the damp from
our sleeping bags, but the discomfort is wearing me down.
There is a black mould growing inside the bag and I have
grit in creases I didn't know I had. But the shallow cave feels
safer, somehow, from the wild boar.

Mrs Campbell turns up eventually, and squeezes in
between May and Arlene, who grumble in their sleep.

The night is long and very scary. Above the waves my
ears pick up the sounds of the jungle: crashing, screeching,
howling. Hope snores through the horrors of darkness. I
have given up trying to read my book after dark. We have
to preserve our torch batteries.

This rash is driving me mad. I can't stop scratching.

Lying there, it occurs to me that we need meat. Protein.
Perhaps we could build a trap. Dig a pit on one of the tracks
the boar use regularly and cover it with branches, or make a
trap with wire. But how would we bait it? Unless we dig up
the body of Natalie or the boatman and use some of their
rotting flesh. Boars eat carrion.

Listen to me! I can't believe I'm considering such awful
things. But it would kill two birds with one stone: rid us

of a dangerous beast and provide us with much-needed protein.

Birds. That's it. We could kill a bird. But we haven't a gun.

How long does it take before starving survivors think seriously about cannibalism? Who would I want to eat? Ugh! No one.

I might try those little ghost crabs, except that it might be like having a large spider in my mouth. I could eat live shrimps. I would even eat raw eggs, if only we could find any.

I go over our list in my head. We have two knives, fishing line and hooks, spears, net. We haven't yet used the hank of net that was washed up.

The sea is high and noisy and the strong wind whines.

Dad has his arms open to me. He is wearing ordinary clothes, not his uniform. He's smiling and I am little again and run to him and leap into his arms, throwing my legs around his waist. But then suddenly I am alone and he is walking away from me, his arms around a woman with long auburn hair—not Mummy.

I wake sobbing.

I feel Jas stirring beside me.

'Bonnie, we're going to get rescued and go home. I can't wait to see my baby brother. I really miss him. Now, close your eyes and let's pretend we're having a sleepover at your house.'

100

I can almost feel the ceiling fan whirring above me. If I reach up I could touch the mosquito net over my bed.

'Do you think your mum might want to take you and Francisco away from Thailand—go back to the States?'

'No, she'd never leave Dad here on his own.'

'Why, doesn't she trust him?'

'God, no, it's not that. Of *course* she trusts him. No, she wouldn't want him to have no one to look after him when he's on leave.'

I hold my tongue about who I reckon is looking after him while she is nursing her migraines. There's no point in upsetting Jas, and anyway I might be totally wrong.

A few hours pass and the night fades gradually. We doze, fitfully. But we never really sleep.

'Come on, we need to get more food.'

We find our shoes and stumble over the other girls. Mrs Campbell has a bare arm flung over Arlene's back. May has still got curlers in her hair. Jas and I giggle at the ridiculous sight.

CHAPTER TWELVE

Day 11, Koh Tabu.
They are looking for us, but in the wrong place.

We see a black spot in the sky, way over by the nearest island to the mainland. It keeps on zigzagging across the island and the channel between that one and the next. A helicopter, but not heading in this direction. Jas and I stoke up the fire, but the damp wood is reluctant to do much more than produce a thin veil of smoke.

'See, Mrs Campbell? They *are* looking for us.'

But they don't appear again.

'You two, help me with this net, will you? It's torn.' I despise the Barbie Babes, but for some reason I can't give up on them. They are sitting on rocks by the sea, May is weaving Mrs Campbell's hair into thin braids.

'No way, hate sewing,' says May.

'Yeah, piss off, spaz lover.' Arlene is applying red lipstick, sticky and dark as blood, the same colour as the woman's lips.

'Let Layla see what I've done with her hair,' says May, snatching at the small rectangular mirror that Arlene is holding.

'Haven't finished with it, *gedoff*.' She goes to grab it back and the mirror falls and smashes on the rocks.

'You stupid bitch. You crazy stupid bitch.'

They hit out at each other, scratching and screeching. Mrs Campbell sits, unmoving and unmoved, as if she is the statue of a goddess.

I retrieve the largest piece of broken mirror from between rocks and leave them to it.

Great! Mrs Campbell is now high on a hallucinogenic plant. That's all we need.

Mrs Campbell has found a new way to escape reality—chewing the seeds of a datura plant. At the forest edge are dozens of small trees covered in the cream trumpet-like too fragrant blooms.

'She was supposed to be looking for food, not drugs,' says Jas, angrily. Now she's lying in the shade of a palm, eyes glazed, red mouth open, a hibiscus blossom rotting in her hair, cheesecloth blouse loosely tied, one breast uncovered, red petticoat torn and grubby, red toe nails chipped and horny. May's hair styling, stiffened with salt and sand, remains intact, despite the wreckage below.

Hope, Jas, and I are wading into the sea at the far end of the beach to our camp. The Portuguese men-o'-war have gone. I try not to think about sharks.

We walk out as far as we can, Hope at one end of the boatman's net, Jas and I at the other. But it keeps floating to the surface.

'We need more weights or something on the bottom edge, so it drags along the bottom,' I call to the others.

After an age of searching we find enough heavy shells with holes in to tie them to the bottom edge of the net. We survey our handiwork proudly.

'That's better,' says Jas. 'Who'd have thought we'd make such expert fishermen!' We wade out again, then gather the net into a smaller and smaller circle as we gradually move closer to the beach. It works. We have caught two beautiful parrotfish—with their large fluorescent scales of bright blue and emerald green. They flap on the rocks while the juniors hit them with sticks and rocks.

'I've never killed anything before,' says Jody. The others jump and scream with excitement. There's a brief moment of happiness before Jas hits her forehead with the palm of her hand. 'How could we be so stupid!' she hisses. 'We haven't any matches. We can't cook the fish.'

Think! Think! Think!

I try to remember movies I've seen with natives making fire. I know Dad's done it. You rub a stick into a split made in another stick, and keep twisting it fast until smoke appears. He says it's harder than it sounds. Much harder. But I've got to give it a go. I end up with aching wrists, blistered hands and no smoke. We all try and fail, even Hope.

'Let's ask Mrs Campbell.'

'You've got to be joking. She's totally out of it.'

Then Hope offers me her one-eye glasses. 'M-m-maybe these will help?'

Yes, of course! In *Lord of the Flies* they used Piggy's broken specs to make fire.

'Brilliant, Hope, what a good idea!' Jas says. 'Actually,

William Golding got it wrong. Piggy had myopia and they wouldn't have been able to use his specs to make fire. We can use yours though.'

Hope smiles.

Jas is such a clever clogs.

But the sun's gone again. Huge dark clouds, like battle-ships, sweep across the sky, sinking lower and lower.

'Oh well, we'll just have to salt them instead. There's lots left,' says Jas.

She sees the bright side of things, whereas I . . . well, I am just angry and fed up and feel as if I could murder someone. I wake angry and go to sleep furious.

Hope and I cut the fish into thin strips. Jas rubs salt on them and then hangs them to dry over the net. Small red flies come from everywhere, attracted by the smell.

We can't wait longer than a couple of hours, we're all so hungry. So we eat the fish, sharing it with the juniors. It's disgusting. But it's protein. And now I can't get rid of the smell of fish on my fingers, no matter how much I wash them. Oh for a bar of soap! I'm sure Dad said there was a leaf you could use as a substitute, but I obviously wasn't listening hard enough when he told me.

'Why are May and Arlene eating leaves?' asks Jody.

'Because they're stupid, and don't you eat any, they're poisonous.'

'Then why are *they* allowed to eat them?'

'They aren't very poisonous to big people,' I lie.

'Oh.'

Mum once told me that Datura gives you nightmares and that you lose control over body functions. So why anyone would want to try it is beyond me.

Later, while we are washing in fresh water, downstream of where we gather drinking water, I suggest to Jas that the juniors see us as the adults now.

'Yes, and Hope, too.'

'What on earth is wrong with that woman?' I mutter, glaring in Mrs Campbell's direction.

'She's just fallen apart. I mean, I think that's what has happened. A breakdown,' Jas says, as she dips her feet into the stream and cleans between her toes.

'What's the Barbie Babes' excuse then?'

'Stupidity? Lack of imagination? They act like this is all a big joke. A laugh.'

Right on cue they come staggering towards us, obviously stoned.

'Layla's *sooo* sick,' says May.

'So are you by the look of you. Why do you take that stuff?' I sound like Mum.

'I only chewed a tiny bit of leaf, Layla ate seeds. Think I'm going to throw up.' May vomited onto the sand in front of us.

'Gross, ugh, gross!' says Arlene and follows suit.

CHAPTER TH1RTEEN

Day 12—I think
I have given up all hope of anyone coming for us. They have
no idea where we are and they probably think we died the first
night. But they would surely be looking for our bodies? If they
are still alive.

I wish I had made notches in a palm trunk every morning,
to help keep count of the days. I feel a real need for order
in my life. Civilization seems to have broken down for us
very quickly. No rituals like cereal for breakfast, no school,
no homework, no lemonade time. No tea and biscuits. No
cleaning of teeth or soap and showers. No clean clothes.
We are simply existing—surviving. We are like a drifting
rudderless boat.

Writing in my journal and reading Mum's book are the
only ways I know to make me feel normal. For a short
time I can forget what's happening to us. The book is in a
bad state—torn and battered, like the journal, with some
pages glued together and the cover bent and swollen. Mum
doesn't even break the spines of her books—it's a point of
pride with her. I grab the book and my journal, find myself
a sheltered place behind a rock, try not to scratch my legs,
and begin to read.

* * *

Zen and the Art of Motorcycle Maintenance is a very unusual book. It's not a novel. It's the story of a journey a man and his young son make across America. The narrator, Phaedrus, is good at maintaining his motorbike but his friends on another bike are not interested in anything technical. They want to float through life without knowing how things work. Phaedrus tries to get his friends interested but they really don't want to know. They get angry when things go wrong and they have to depend on professional mechanics' help to get them out of trouble. He doesn't. He doesn't let his bike's condition deteriorate. He spends evenings oiling the parts and twiddling with spark plugs and brakes and stuff, adjusting the engine so it works well and doesn't let him down.

But something else is happening in the story. He is revisiting his past—the college where he worked as a teacher and had some sort of breakdown. But somehow this means that he is in danger of breaking down again. He remembers how his thoughts took him to a point of no return, and he is getting dangerously closer to the truth that drove him over the edge of sanity.

It seems to be about philosophy too, about Art against Science, and how they could work together. But most arty people can't change a fuse, and most science people can't appreciate poetry—that's a simplification but Mum says it's more or less right.

I think I am a practical, science-y person. I like to know how things work. I like taking things apart and putting them together again—like radios and clocks and locks. But should I try to be an art person too? I can see how lovely things are: appreciate sunsets and rainbows and things like that. I particularly like finding different ways to describe colours.

But I also need to know why the colours are there, why a bird has bright tail feathers or why a butterfly has an eye painted on its wing. I don't simply accept the world and go WOW! I need to know why it is wow-ish and wow-some. That's just the way I am. Anyway, I do like drawing and writing poems so I am slightly arty. Once—it seems like years ago—Mrs Campbell asked to see some of my poems.

I don't know how any of that is going to help me in this situation. I'm fit, and I can run and climb and swim quite well, so those skills might help. We'll see.

It's only a matter of time before they find us . . . isn't it? I can't bring myself to believe Mrs Campbell's theory about the explosions. The Vietcong can't have attacked Thailand. Our forces are stronger than theirs—we're always being told that on the news and in the newspapers. The Americans and allies are going to win the war.

Maybe there were lightning strikes on the base and things are taking a long time to sort out. Everything is so laid back in Thailand; everything takes time here. Mum reckons it's part of the country's charm but Dad gets ratty when things don't work and we have to wait ages to get them fixed. That's where I come in. I often fix things at the house—like the plumbing. There was a blockage somewhere and they couldn't get a plumber to come. There was such a bad smell! A land crab had got stuck in the drain outlet for the bath and died. I found and removed it and saved them hundreds of *baht*. Even Dad was impressed.

Lots of people are like Dad, and get fed up with the way the Thais take their time over everything. That's why so many military families live on the base at Utapao. It's like a little piece of America. I'm glad we don't. I like being part of Thai life. For example, one of the charcoal burner's daughters at Amnuythip is a really good dancer. We've watched her perform in the *Lakhon* dance-drama at the local *wat*. Her hands are like charmed snakes, writhing and twisting. She's very supple. We'd miss out on that kind of thing if we lived on the base.

Life should be *sanuk*—fun—they say. People smile a lot.

I have a sudden horrific image in my head of Lek's children in flames, screaming and running naked, unable to escape the fire that consumes them.

I wonder if Americans are making things worse for the Thais? Involving them in the war? Encouraging their daughters to be prostitutes—after all, they can earn far more working as bar girls than they could helping their mamas grow rice.

I see the point of the Peace Movement, I certainly do . . . But as a USAF employee's child I have to toe the line. My fights with Dad are almost always about the war. He shouts at me. I don't listen. I shout at him. He doesn't listen. Mum says we are so like each other. I think we are opposites. And if a man and his daughter can't keep the peace why should the North and South Vietnamese? He took my CND badge and threw it in the garbage. I was singing along to Dylan . . .

'Yes, 'n' how many deaths will it take till he knows
That too many people have died?'

110

I told him that if every soldier refused to fight there'd be no war. But Dad said there are some things we have to fight for, like freedom of speech. But why do we have to fight in a country far from home? So what if part of that country wants the other part to be communists? Dad said it isn't as simple as that. And he got really mad and went out and slammed the door.

Our arguments upset Mum, I know.

My mind is alive with ideas and questions. I open the journal and my pencil hovers above the paper. What can I write?

May 20? 1974 The island.
Day 12?
Dear Mum and Dad,
If I don't survive and you eventually find this journal, please know I love you both and I'm sorry if I've been a trouble to you. I'm sorry, Dad, that I always argue with you. I'm sorry. I wish I could be home with you. I wish you weren't in the war, Daddy. I pray you are both safe. I love you both. xxx
Your loving daughter, Bonnie.
Please tell Grandma and Grandpa I love them too.

It's not much, but it says what I think is most important for them to know.

CHAPTER FOURTEEN

Koh Tabu—still
Day 12
All we do is try to keep dry, and not go hungry. We're not successful at either.
   I've decided to attempt to fix the outboard motor.

The first thing we do is dig a small fresh-water pool down-stream of where we gather our drinking water. It's vital that we don't contaminate our life-saving water source.

That done, with Hope's formidable strength we shift the outboard motor from the sand up to the pool. She thinks she's fixed it by drying it out by the fire but I'm hoping that by dunking it in fresh water we will rinse out all the corrosive salt water.

'Let's s-s-see if there's any f-f-fuel left first.' Hope angles a plastic water can underneath. She unscrews the fuel tank and tips up the machine. A trickle of petrol slips out and into the empty water can. There's about half a gallon.

'Good,' I tell her. 'Now let's lift it into the pool.'

Exhausted from the effort, we leave it for a few hours before hoisting it out and placing it on a work-bench made from three palm trunks shoved close together. That was another of Hope's ideas.

'What would we do without you, Hope?' says Jas, breathlessly.

'N-n-now what?' Hope looks at me.

'Now I take the motor apart and clean the components and put them together again.'

'What g-g-good will that d-do?'

'What do you mean?'

Jas sits on the sand looking whacked.

'When I strip it down I'll discover what's wrong and put it right.'

Somewhere a gibbon laughs derisively and his entire family join in.

My Swiss army knife has thirteen features:

1. Large blade
2. Small blade
3. Can opener
4. Small screwdriver
5. Bottle opener
6. Large screwdriver
7. Wire stripper
8. Reamer/punch—I've no idea what it's for.
9. Wood-saw
10. Corkscrew
11. Tweezers
12. Toothpick
13. Keyring

I haven't used any of them before apart from the wood-saw, can opener, toothpick and tweezers (I have a problem with my eyebrows—they nearly meet in the middle, or would do if they had their own way) and the large blade.

The big screwdriver is ideal for the main screws on the motor. Well, not ideal, but it'll do. My fingers are sore very quickly.

'Hope, could you have a try?'

'Sure, let me at it.'

She has a good strong grip and she definitely has more patience than me. I note the parts in my journal in the order we dismantle them. I'm methodical. I write numbers on scraps of my notepaper and label each motor part, just the way Phaedrus would have done.

'This is a lot of effort for what?'

'Jas, don't be dense. For our survival. For our escape, for goodness' sake.'

'Yes but we'll never build anything strong enough to take the weight of the motor.'

'If you don't want to help, fine. Leave me to do it alone.'

They watch me without comment as I struggle to undo one small screw. I have ruined the thread of it now, the notch is ragged and too big for the little screwdriver.

Hope suggests a nail file. May has one.

'Go and ask her for it, then.'

'N-n-no, I c-c-can't, you go.'

'You go,' I insist. My voice is savage.

'I'll go,' says Jas. She gives me a look. She does this, Jas. She never says anything, but you know when she disapproves of something you've said or done. Hope and I sit and look at the waves rolling in, the huge surf breaking on the reef, saying nothing. I'm so tired and hungry. I feel like crying.

'Madam isn't happy,' says Jas and hands me the metal file.

'Is she ever?'

It snaps as soon as I try to twist it in the groove of the screw.

'It's useless. Shit, shit, *shit*!' I lose it completely, kicking the motor, and throw the nail file into the sand.

Day 13

We made a decision in the night—Jas, Hope, and me. At first light Jas and I are going inland. We reckon that if we get to the highest peak in the west and can make fire there, build a bonfire, the smoke will be seen from further away. We'll get rescued.

I think my toe may be broken but I'm determined to make the trip.

I feel so much better, now that we've decided to take matters into our own hands. Hope will stay behind and keep watch over Carly and Jody. I don't trust the others to look after themselves let alone the juniors. She offers to stay. It makes sense, as she can't see to climb very well. Also I think she is becoming fond of the juniors and enjoys the way they look up to her.

I wake Jody.

'We're going to get help for us all,' I tell her. 'Be good, now, stay in the shade and drink lots of water. There's plenty of coconut milk and nut, already cut up. Eat it.'

She looks at me sleepily.

'Is Jas going? Don't go, don't leave me.' She begins to whimper.

115

I hug her. 'We won't be long. Hope will look after you.'

We leave at dawn, a cloudy cool dawn with storm clouds piling up, all angry orange-brown and purple. The sea is broiling from the incessant wind, even in the lagoon. On the reef waves crash and tumble in a wide white frill. I would hate to be in a boat on that.

Maybe a helicopter will come for us, if they can spare a helicopter. Maybe they can't spare military personnel to come looking for a group of overdue girl cadets.

It's good to walk in the cool of the morning. We take my bag containing salt, coconut, Hope's broken glasses, a towel, my journal and pencil, book and flashlight. The rolled up sleeping bags are slung over our shoulders and the water bottles shared between us.

For kindling we have gathered some of the hairy sacking stuff that grows at the top of the coconut palm. There are plenty of fallen palms. We'll find twigs and fire material when we get there. We have my Swiss army knife and we each have spears.

Once in the jungle it's dark and damply sticky; we keep tripping over tree roots. My toe is still painful but I am not admitting it. We strip off our sweat-shirt sleeves and wrap the material over and around our exposed ankles.

We pass through a plantation of thick bamboos, clanking and clinking loudly in the wind.

'They're like enormous wind-chimes,' says Jas. Then we reach into evergreen forest, strewn with trees felled in the storm.

'Look, gibbon!' Jas points to the little face watching from a high branch. He leaps away, whooping and screeching. Branches bend and swoosh and wave. Other gibbons take up the call and we hear them screaming at each other. It must be the gibbons we've been hearing in the night. They're renowned for their songs. Sometimes the loudest noise in the forest is the song of gibbons. Families like a sing-song, Jas tells me, but then one will sing a solo and the others will listen. Or we'll hear a duet—love songs, I reckon. We stand and watch for a little while.

'They are amazingly agile even though they have no tails. And their arms are twice the length of their bodies,' Jas tells me.

We follow a narrow trail.

'Wild boar?' suggests Jas.

'I suppose so. It must be quite large.' I'd rather not think about it, remembering Dad's experience. 'Let's hope we don't meet one coming our way.'

The path is about two feet wide and although we have to bend and stoop to get under branches it isn't too difficult. Yet. Where we try to get off the track we find the forest impenetrable. I have unravelled part of the towel and made ribbons to tie on bushes every so often so we can find our way back. Like Hansel and Gretel and the crumbs.

Resting for a moment on a rock I am suddenly covered in red ants.

'Help! I'm being bitten to death.' Jas helps me brush them off.

'Better the red ones than the black. They really hurt.'

I get out the map I made on our first trip into the interior.

'Look, Jas, the highest point in the western mountain is about five miles away. We should do that in a day easily.'

'Five miles!'

We have a swig of water. Strange bird calls, high branches creaking in the wind, insects squeaking and tapping and scratching; monkeys hoo-hooing and coughing. It's never quiet in the forest. In the distance the sea rolling past the island, a sea that breathes and is totally alien: it doesn't care about anything, but exists, as we do.

'What's that?' A scratching and swishing of branches behind us—a wild boar? My heart is in my mouth.

Then comes a sharp yelp.

'What are you doing? *Jody!* I told you to stay in camp.'

She gets up from where she has tripped and emerges from the bushes, her thin legs scratched and bleeding, her T-shirt with its orange smiley face covered in mud.

She goes to Jas and hugs her.

'Mikey said we had to come with you.'

'Mikey is a damned nuisance,' I say, and she starts crying.

'Oh come on now. We'll put up with Mikey and you,' Jas says gently and offers her a drink of water.

I'm outraged. 'Be serious, Jas, we can't take her with us. It might be dangerous.'

'She's here now. We can't send her back.'

Jody drinks greedily. 'I've brought Teddy,' she says. 'I couldn't leave him behind.'

That's all we need: a wee kid, a teddy bear, and a bossy invisible buddy.

Suddenly, out of nowhere, a king cobra, about ten feet long, appears, its head raised to the height of Jody's face, not six feet away from her. We freeze. Silently the huge creature, its hood spread in a death threat, strikes. The smaller brown-black snake, which we had not noticed on the leafy track before us is paralysed almost immediately and we watch, fascinated, as the huge snake slowly swallows it before slithering away to disappear into the thick undergrowth.

'Did that really happen or did I imagine it?' I am shaking.

'Mikey doesn't like snakes,' whispered Jody, clinging to her teddy.

'I don't blame him.' Jas hugs her and then goes into 'fascinating fact mode'. 'They have neurotoxins in their venom, that's what paralyses the prey. A king cobra delivers more venom per bite than any other kind of cobra—enough to kill twenty people.'

'Yeah, thanks for the chemistry lesson, Jas. I feel much better now.' I'm still annoyed that we have Jody slowing us down. 'Come on. We need to get on.'

'Did you notice its eyes?'

'What?'

'Cobras have round pupils, not vertical.'

I set off, refusing to be drawn into a discussion about snake eyes.

We hack our way through the difficult bits, where whatever it was that made the path has tunnelled under rather than through the bush.

'We can't *crawl* across the island, for goodness' sake,' I complain.

Jas gives Jody a piggyback where the path widens and clears, but then she has to manage on her own as we climb gradually. The limestone rocks are rounded and it's fairly easy to clamber over them. When Jody can't make it I climb first and Jas pushes her up to me.

We've made Jody's shirtsleeves into socks to protect her legs.

'Oh, look, it's so pretty.' Jody goes to touch a blue lizard on a rock.

Jas grabs her hand away. 'No, don't touch. Its skin might excrete deadly chemicals.'

'What's excrete?'

'Just don't touch anything, OK?' I explode.

She goes quiet after that and I feel guilty for shouting. Poor kid, she's only ten or something and her sister's just died.

'You know, we were very lucky that king cobra didn't chase us.' Jas is trying to chivvy me back into a better temper.

'Chase us?' I play along.

'Yeah, they are really aggressive snakes, run after people for miles to bite them.'

'You're kidding me?'

'Nope, they really do.'

Jody's eyes are like saucers. There's no way she'll risk touching anything or being left behind now.

Jas knows all sorts of stuff about animals. Sometimes it's better not to know.

Lianas tangle everything and we have to decide every time whether to climb over or under them. Every small peak reveals many more, each covered in forest undergrowth and tall trees, of every green I've ever seen and a few more besides. Leaves are of every shape possible for a leaf to be: round, heart shaped, long and thin, spear-like, hairy, prickly. I'd love to collect samples but there isn't time.

We must pass a dozen or so different sorts of bamboo. Thin black stemmed, thick brown stemmed, thorny.

All the time flies settle on our sweaty faces and arms. They bite.

'Ouch!' Jody slaps at herself and laughs. On we march, slithering downhill and scrambling uphill, pulling ourselves up by hanging on to stems and trunks. There's no way we could camp here. Jas keeps up a commentary on the wildlife we hear—squabbling squirrels, croaking frogs, drilling of cicadas. We pass jungle trees strangled by figs and ferns and orchids growing on every available tree bark, spaghetti junctions of lianas, pushing their way up towards the light. Some palms have nasty spikes. Too late, Jas warns me that some of the leaves sting if you touch them.

'This is not a friendly forest,' she says, as she helps tie another ribbon to a tree.

We come at last to a natural clearing, surrounded by thick trees, with several large flattish rocks, and we're blinded by light after the gloom of jungle. Sunshine, no wind.

'Here's good for a camp,' says Jas.

'OK, it'll do,' I agree. I wish we'd gone further but have to admit that Jody hasn't kept us back. I don't know how far we've travelled but we're hot and thirsty and need food. We share out the coconut and water.

Jas knows I'm disappointed. 'It's still a while until sunset but this is such a good place and we might not find anything better further on,' she puts a hand on my shoulder. 'Shall we try and light a fire?'

'Is there any point?'

'Well, to keep wild animals away. And be a comfort.'

'OK.'

121

I'm in charge of fire-making. I place some of my precious supply of tinder—lichens and coconut hair—in a small heap on a rock. I hold the remaining lens of Hope's broken glasses close to the kindling and angle it to catch the sun's low rays. There is a slight acrid smell and my tinder sparks.

'Yes, fire! We have fire!'

Jas and Jody peer closely.

'Where? Can't see it.'

'Go find more twigs.'

'OK, keep your hair on.'

Slightly larger twigs go on next then larger ones, dried leaves and bark. But it's all too damp and the fire smoulders briefly before fading to nothing. I blow gently on it but there's nothing . . . no smoke, no fire.

'Never mind, it's good practice,' says Jas briskly.

'But what about wild animals?' whines Jody.

'Ssh, now, get in my sleeping bag and don't worry. We'll keep watch. Nothing's going to hurt you. I promise.'

'Will you promise nothing's going to hurt *me*, please, Mummy?' I whisper and Jas slaps me and giggles.

At dusk come the fruit bats, first one or two, then a dozen or more, then in their hundreds they flock to roost upside down in the dark trees. The rustling of batwings surrounds us.

'Hope probably had forty fits worrying about where Jody is.'

'Jas, stop worrying. There's nothing we can do about it. You should have let me send Jody back when we first found her.'

Her silence is loud.

As night falls fireflies come—thousands of them above our heads, all flashing together in a constant rhythm, like a nightclub light show. Later there are green glow-worms, and a marvellous glowing fungus that grows on logs, creating the most exotic join-the-dots puzzle.

At one point there is the rustle of leaves behind us. I shine the torch beam on a little deer, which staggers off in terror.

The idea was for Jas to take first watch while Jody and I slept. Then I would take the second watch at midnight while Jas slept in my sleeping bag. But in the end Jas and I both keep watch together, as I can't sleep.

'Do you think there might be tigers here, Jas?'

'Well, it's a largish island and there are plenty of small animals—dhole, you know—a sort of wild dog—and mousedeer . . .'

'We haven't seen those have we?'

'No, they look like rabbits on stilts—they're bound to be here—and pheasants, I think, and jacanas, wild boar, of course, and loads of monkeys and gibbons, and rats—they have from four to seven litters a year—and barking deer, that's what we saw earlier and I think they're a Thai tiger's main prey—so enough available for a big cat, I suppose. So yes, I suppose there could be a tiger.'

'And if there's one, there's bound to be more.'

There's a silence, and I'm suddenly aware of the pressure that Jas puts herself under to remain cheerful at all times.

'Oh, Bonnie, perhaps we should have stayed on the beach. What if we can't even get the fire lit?'

'Too late to think of that now. We'll just have to hope for the best.'

Are we going to die? How will it feel to be attacked by a wild beast, torn apart, to bleed to death? No one will ever find our remains here. Our dismembered parts will be dined on by ants, our bones will bleach and crumble over the years. An archaeologist of the future will find a broken toe bone and wonder what happened to the rest of the body.

My school teachers often tell me I have an overactive imagination. I wonder if they'd say so now.

I shine the torch all around us but we see nothing. Just trees and leaves and bushes. No glinting eyes. Jody sleeps. I turn off the light reluctantly.

'Jas, talk to me. Talk to me.'

'What about?'

'Uh, tell me what you did before you came to Thailand.'

'Before? Well, Dad was at a pilot-training camp in Nevada. Mom and me were miles away. Mum had a psychology practice in the city. My baby brother wasn't born then. Uh, I went to junior high, had a crush on my biology teacher, wore braces, the usual stuff. You?'

'Borneo before here. I loved it, except it rained a lot, and we didn't see much of Dad, but before that we lived in Scotland, which is where I was born, and that's almost as wet. But I was just a little kid then.'

'What's it like, Scotland? It sounds so romantic and exotic.'

'I remember snow and icy roads, and going to school on a bus and my white breath. Icicles on the windows. Building a snowman in the garden.'

We sit quietly listening to the night. Jody stirs, cries out 'No!' but she's still asleep. Jas strokes her head.

Then Jas says, 'Mom and Dad were much happier then, when she was working. They came with me to spelling bees and we'd go to baseball games together. We don't seem to do anything as a family any more.'

'Were you always good at spelling?'

'Yeah, won the Nevada State Championship twice.'

'Wow!' We are both quiet for a moment then I ask, 'Don't you think they are happy now then?'

'No, not really. It's the war, isn't it? Who can be happy when there's the constant threat of death?'

'Yeah, I suppose.' I think how lucky I am that my parents are still happy together—as far as I know. They cuddle a lot, embarrassingly so, and talk to each other. They dance together at base parties. I don't know what I'd do if they ever wanted to separate. I couldn't possibly choose who I'd live with, even though I'm not getting on with Dad at the moment.

'Will you go back to Scotland when the war is over?'

'When the war is over . . . and if we get off this island . . . *when* we get off this island—yeah, I suppose so. That's the plan. Depends on where Daddy is sent. Mum likes to go where he goes if it's longer than six months. But my grandparents, Dad's parents, live in Sutherland—that's in the north of Scotland. They used to live in Caithness and I lived with them for a while, went to my first school there—and we often go to them in the holidays. We stay in their guest cottage, which used to be stables, and they have a little rowing boat, and highland cattle with shaggy brown coats and tall horns. You'd love it. There are eagles and ospreys and a loch.' We laugh together at my Scottish pronunciation. 'Perhaps you could come and stay?'

Just thinking about my grandparents makes me want to cry.

It's 1964. My parents are away somewhere, probably in a war zone. I am four years old and living with Grandma and Grandpa, and in this memory I'm walking with them across the purple brown moor of Dunnet Head in Caithness, further north than John O'Groats, but a few miles to the east.

I follow in Grandpa's footsteps, and Grandma treads in mine. If I don't exactly tread in his footprints she warns I might disappear for ever into a bottomless bog. Grandma's full of horror stories. Just before my arrival a young man died gathering seagull eggs from the cliff face. The fall is 300 feet into a churning sea.

'He never stood a chance,' she says, gleefully.

We are coming back from the little kirk in the hamlet of Brough, Grandpa in his black serge coastguard uniform with gold braid on his cap and Grandma dressed in black. I am all wrapped up in tweed coat, woollen scarf, and Fair Isle tam', my feet tingling from the cold in knitted socks that have slipped under my heels in the black wellington boots. Ice sits like hand mirrors on puddles in the blackened heather. There's a mossy patch that Grandpa skirts but I decide to take a more direct route. I start to walk across the bright green stuff, feeling sponge, crunchy from frost, give under my feet.

'No, lassie.' Grandpa grabs me and I think he is saving me from a bottomless bog. But he's not. 'Never walk on the moss. It's very fragile, you see. The first time it will survive; the second it doesn't spring back up; if someone walks on it a third time the moss will die. And you wouldn't want that, would you now?'

No, I wouldn't want that.

I wipe my damp eyes with my arm. 'It's a lovely place, Jas, no trees, just lakes and cliffs, the empty moor, and seabird cries.'

'It sounds so foreign, Bonnie.'

'It's home, sort of, or was, when I was little.'

We sit quietly for a while, deep in our own thoughts.

'What do you think went wrong with Mrs Campbell?'

'What I said before, Bonz. She's given up trying to be in control because she's in shock. Everything's out of control. The storm; Sandy; the boatman; Natalie—three deaths. She doesn't know what's hit her. And she's supposed to be in charge. She just isn't up to it.'

'You're being too kind, Jas. She's not in shock, no more than we are, anyway. And she's a liar. What survival skills has she shown? Nothing. And she drank the whisky, two bottles nearly, instead of using it to clean Natalie's leg. And she's encouraging Arlene and May to smoke marijuana and eat druggy leaves. That's corruption of minors.' I've read that phrase in a newspaper.

'I suppose you're right.'

We say nothing.

I am filled again with the fury I can't express. Every time I think of Layla Campbell I want to be sick.

Jody sleeps the sleep of the innocent, as does Mikey presumably.

We see our first army of termites. The winged insects

127

cover the forest floor as far as we can see. I wonder if they're attracted by the light? Dad says you can eat termites but you have to pull off the wings first and eat them raw or cook them. Full of protein, apparently.

What sounds like hundreds of tree frogs have settled on tree trunks around us and make a noise like a spoon on a teacup—*chink* . . . pause . . . *chink, chink* . . . pause . . . *chink, chink, chink*. They're very clever. They count to five then start all over again. I listen carefully to see if they ever count higher than five, but they don't. I am in danger of falling asleep counting not sheep but frog chirps.

Eventually Jas wriggles down, trying to make herself as comfy a bed as she can. 'I have to sleep, Bonz. Sorry.' Her breathing steadies almost immediately.

I don't know how long it is before I hear a strange new sound, a cross between a loud sigh and a sort of roar. My blood goes cold. I've always wondered what that expression meant and now I know. That wasn't a wild boar. I turn the torch on and wave it around but can see nothing but red eyes high in the trees—monkeys or gibbons. I edge my journal out from beneath Jas's sleeping body.

I really liked Mrs Campbell when we first met her. I feel like I've been fooled, cheated, let down. I feel ashamed of her because she's from Scotland and she's so immoral. And what if I'm right about that day in the car? Maybe Mum's friends are right not to trust her.

This isn't turning out to be the journal I had imagined taking home with me.

CHAPTER FIFTEEN

Day 14
Still alive. Not eaten in the night.

I wake the others.

'Not much of a hotel, this,' I joke, as the others come to their senses. 'No barbecue or campfire, no bacon roll or waffles with maple syrup, no fresh orange juice; no smell of freshly brewed coffee, no hot shower, no room service.'

'It's a disgrace,' agrees Jas. 'We won't be back.'

Jody smiles shyly, happy to be with us.

'It's the mundane things I miss the most,' says Jas. 'What I'd give for a good night's sleep, toilet tissue, clean underwear . . . '

'The inside of my mouth tastes like a cave full of bat crap,' I say.

'Mine tastes like a garbage bin,' complains Jas.

'Mine's worse. It tastes like dog poo!' Jody is delighted with herself, and we all laugh. The first laugh any of us have had for a long time.

We are on our way at dawn. No point in hanging around.

'Look at the ants, Jody.'

'What are they carrying?'

'Leaves. Bigger than they are.'

Jody screams. 'A snake!' Her scream sets off the gibbons whose yells and whoops fill the forest. 'No it isn't, sorry, it's a tree root.'

If we stop for a rest or a drink any exposed flesh gets stung by ants so small we can hardly see them, so we try to keep moving, climbing. It's not actually raining. Instead a low mist clings to the trees, a thick whiteness dampens our hair and skin. Everything is clammy. But gradually, as the sun rises, the mist breaks into tatters and thin streaks thread their way into the coral red morning sky.

Jody's a gutsy little thing. She seems to think this is a great adventure. She's tanned and dirty all over and her face is covered in mud, her hair tangled and stuck with leaves. She doesn't notice the thorns. Her teddy is in my bag. She hasn't once mentioned her sister, but maybe that's not a good thing.

Having a crap in the jungle isn't easy. We can't go off into the forest for privacy in case we lose each other or come across another snake. We dig a shallow bowl with our hands in the leafy muddy earth and crouch, use a big leaf to clean ourselves and cover our waste with leaves and earth. The other two keep watch from close by.

Jody holds her nose and goes 'Disgusting, ugh, yuck!' And I have to agree.

'Look, a pill bug!' Jas gives us little zoology and biology lectures. This particular tank-like bug trundles around on the forest floor and when disturbed curls up to look like a conker. You can't see where the segments of its armour begin and end, it is so beautifully engineered.

We gather fruit whenever we come across it. There's a banana grove at one point and we have bananas for breakfast and carry as many as we can to eat later.

'I wonder what's happening back at the beach?' Jas munches her way through one of the remaining bananas.

'Yeah, have the Barbie Babes scratched each other's eyes out yet? Is Hope hanging on in there, looking after Carly? Has Loopy Layla pulled herself together?'

'Who's Loopy Layla?' asks Jody, wiping sticky spider's web from her face.

We are gradually getting higher and the path is all rocky now, no leaf floor, no actual track to follow any more. It's a matter of climbing upwards until we reach the top.

We've eaten all the bananas. They don't travel well. And we've seen no other fruit for ages, though we can hear gibbons nearby so there must be something for them to eat.

There's so many different fruits in the market at home—durian, custard apple, jackfruit, papaya, pineapple, pomello, rambutan, breadfruit, mangosteen and watermelon. I'll never take them for granted again.

But we still have plenty of water, even with an extra stomach to fill.

It's getting hotter. I'm sweating like mad and finding it difficult to breathe. The air is like cotton wool.

A large male gibbon stoops from his branch to stare at us, and not believing his big eyes he shrieks at us.

'Look!' I point out his mate creeping away whooping and wailing in alarm, a baby clasped about her waist. There must be more gibbons here than any other creature.

'Are we there yet?'

Jas and I laugh.

'What?'

I say, 'I can't believe you took so long to ask that, Jody.'

We carry on upwards until we reach the edge of a clearing. Trees here are thin and broken, blackened, some of them, maybe from a lightning strike. In the soft mud are scratch marks and paw prints. It must be a salt or mineral lick.

'We are lucky not to have disturbed anything big feeding here.' Jas peers at the paw prints. 'Maybe we frightened them off.'

Jody is delighted by the yellow butterflies fluttering down to the mud like tickertape from a tall building.

We rest again to get our breath in the welcome cool of a narrow cave mouth, but not for long once Jas has identified a hornets' nest in the roof. We get to our feet, and are just beginning to move out of the cave in single file, me in front, Jody in the middle, when Jas leans forward to grab my arm and I nearly stumble.

'Look!' she squeaks.

A big cat frowns at us from about twenty feet away, so well camouflaged, black stripes merging with the trees. She's huge. Like a dark red pony.

'What is it? I can't see anything,' says Jody in a normal voice, and the tiger turns and lopes away downhill, her enormous paws thudding on the rocks.

'A tiger! We've seen a tiger.' My voice has disappeared into the top of my head.

132

'Do you know that poem, "Tyger, tyger burning bright"?' Jas whispers. 'She did look like she was burning, didn't she? As if there was fire under her skin?' Her eyes are full as if she's about to cry.

'I saw another one,' says Jody.

'What, where?'

'Over there, where your tiger went. It was orange.'

'You imagined it, Jody.'

'No I didn't. It was floating and very tall.'

I sigh. A real tiger is enough to have to deal with without one of Jody's imaginary versions.

'OK.' There's no point in arguing.

We'll have to be even more careful now. Once again, I wish we hadn't got Jody to take care of. If the tiger had seen a small child, God knows what would have happened. The fact that there are tigers here changes everything.

Fear turns my sweat sour.

We are all moving more carefully, constantly looking around. Jody is round-eyed with excitement.

CHAPTER SIXTEEN

Day 14—probably
Month—May
Date—26, or thereabouts
Year—1974
Place—An island somewhere in the Gulf of Thailand.
We are on an island with tigers!

We have stopped for a rest on a boulder and as the rain has stopped I take the opportunity to update the map. No ants, thank goodness. We can see the summit. It's still a long way away, about two hours more I reckon. First we have to get beyond a huge bare rock, or rocky hill, rounded but steep sided, like a beached whale. I think I can make it up, but Jas is dubious and says we'll have to skirt the rock, go the long way round. We're getting short of water and coconut and there's nothing I recognize as edible fruit here. Our sweatshirt 'socks' are shredded and torn.

'My scratches hurt and there's no space on my arms for any more bites.' Even Jas is miserable.

'I could go on alone to build the fire. I don't mind.' I am actually quite reluctant to do it on my own, as a fire needs constant feeding, and more than one pair of hands to gather sticks to feed it.

'No, don't do that, it's getting late.' The voice of sanity speaks and I'm secretly quite relieved.

'OK. Let's camp here and finish the climb tomorrow.'

'I don't want to stay here, I don't like it.'

'What do you mean, you don't like it? What's wrong with here?'

'Mikey doesn't like it.' Jody, who has been so brave, suddenly collapses in a heap and sobs. I feel her brow. She's feverish.

'I want Natalie . . . Natalie . . . where's Natalie?'

Jas and I cry with the poor wee thing for her dead sister, and if we are honest, for ourselves. And once we've started, there's no stopping us.

After dosing her with salt and water we take turns to give Jody piggybacks. We're all exhausted. Maybe she has malaria. We've been bitten enough times. Or dengue fever. The anti-mozzie spray ran out days ago. I think longingly of my lost mosquito coil, useless anyway without matches.

We have to keep resting and drinking water. We'll have to ration it now until we find more. Jody is unable to walk.

'Honestly, Jas. Let me go on alone,' I plead. 'This is going to take for ever.' But she's having none of it, insisting on carrying Jody. Perhaps if we find a decent place for them both to sit, she'll change her mind.

Our Hansel and Gretel ribbons have nearly run out. I've had to halve them in size today so that we won't run out. I keep looking around to take note of landmarks to remember on our descent. Things like a lightning-split tree and a particularly tall palm; that huge rocky mound. As we climb the rocks are more prominent, and steeper sided, and it becomes impossible to get out the map and fill in the details.

135

Cicadas chirp non-stop and are so loud we cannot hear each other speak. My head feels as if it's going to split open.

We can smell the overpowering sweetness of the flowers before we come across a little bush of green lemons or limes. Oh, the freshness of the harsh sharp juice! We squeeze some into Jody's mouth and she shudders at the taste.

'We won't get scurvy anyway,' says Jas, squeezing the contents of one of the fruits into her open mouth. Then suddenly she sits bolt upright. 'Listen!'

'What is it?' My heart is pumping hard.

'Water, I hear water. And I can smell it,' says Jas.

It's the most wonderful sight. A waterfall drops about twenty feet into a rocky pool and black water slithers over pebbles into a stream. We all fall to our knees and drink then paddle in the pool. The water stings my scratched legs but its freshness soothes. Close to the stream there's a flattish rock surrounded by fallen trees.

I try again. 'This looks like a good place to camp. You could look after Jody here while I carry on.'

Jas gives in eventually.

'I don't want to leave you either but it's necessary. If I don't build a fire that can be seen while the weather's clearer, we've got no chance of ever getting off this island.'

We don't say as much but we've chosen a place with no dense cover close by for a tiger to hide in. They have a spear, my Swiss army knife, water and salt, coconut, limes, Jas's torch and a sleeping bag. We agree that they will spend the night on the rock and that Jas will take Jody back to the beach at daylight if she's well enough. I'll check to see if they've gone on my way down.

'I'm going to crack this fire business,' I assure them. 'You'll hear it crackling and sparking, and you'll smell the wood-smoke and see the flames. I won't be far behind you.'

I have the rucksack, which I have filled with tinder material—hairy lichens, coconut husk, and small twigs in case there is nothing suitable at the summit—my own torch and my spear.

I say, 'See you later, alligator.'

'In a while, crocodile.' Jas smiles bravely.

I hope they'll be all right. I refuse to think about tigers. No point in worrying about things that haven't happened.

My plan is to build a fire on the summit and light it before sunset, which is about three hours away. I'll stay there tonight and get back to the beach in the morning.

Steam swirls around the tops of the trees. There's plenty of rotten timber, anyway. I snap off twigs and branches from fallen dead trees. But then I think it's a waste of energy and I should wait until I reach the fire site before I gather material. The jungle thins out here, and there are more low bushes and ferns in the clearings. I find a small fig tree that the gibbons haven't discovered and gather as many figs as I can. I throw out the wood to make room for the fruit.

I can hear a trickling, and follow the sound back into thicker forest. The sound of fresh water has become like a magnet to me. I pass strangely shaped boulders—some might even have been carved to look like animals and huge human heads. I'm glad it's not dark; they'd be scary in the dark. I squeeze between two tall rocks and find a perfect little waterfall—tinkling down from a crevice onto a concave bowl-like rock. I replenish my water bottle, admiring the huge green and red dragonflies and swallowtail butterflies that are hovering in the flow or sipping from the spray, and take the opportunity to wash all over and wet my hair. The water is deliciously icy.

Refreshed, I gaze around me and slowly realize that I am at the entrance to a man-made building of some sort. Hidden by the trees are tall columns of stone, crudely carved, almost covered by climbers. I clamber over fallen columns, also carved with figures. They are difficult to make out but I recognize a giant figure with tusks. It could be a *Yaksha*, a temple guardian with flames carved at its calves and ears. This must be an abandoned *wat*, a temple of some sort. Jas would know. I make my way over roots and under low branches into the centre of the abandoned temple and come across a reclining figure of Buddha. It is about twenty feet long. I scratch the pale honey-coloured surface, wondering if the colour is from gold leaf. But no, it doesn't mark. Which means it could be . . . solid gold. Gold! I've never seen a Buddha lying in this position before. His head is resting on his right hand. His eyes are rubies, I'm sure of it. Most of his body is covered by roots and tree branches, strangling fig and fern. His feet are placed on top of each other neatly, and his toes are painted red.

I feel like falling to my knees and praying, but a gentle rustling nearby makes me jump. A pheasant-like bird emerges, scratching the leaf litter for beetles or seeds. He has a red head and greyish back feathers with a long curved black tail. He ignores me totally.

Maybe I am a figment of his imagination or he is a figment of mine?

I try to take in all the detail so that I can record it in my journal later. I'll name it *Wat of the Golden Buddha*. This must be how Darwin or Alfred Russell Wallace felt. (Mum has this really good travel book by Alfred Russell Wallace called *The Malay Archipelago*. He collected thousands of hitherto unkown species of natural history specimens. I've only read bits of it, but it's brilliant.)

I feel so excited, so lucky. I can't wait to tell the others. I even think—for a split second—of abandoning the plan to build a fire and hurrying back to the camp.

My eyes are getting used to the gloom when something red catches my eye close to the ground. Hanging limp on a spiny rattan is Sandy's red neckerchief. My spirits plummet. I remove the cotton bandana. It has dark brown stains on it. Blood of course. Sandy's blood.

I peer into the darkness of the thick forest. Something is coming this way. My heart's in my throat.

What do I do?

I stand like an idiot, rooted to the spot, while a wild boar ambles past me, not ten yards away, nose to the ground, grunting and farting, its small tusks gleaming in the green of the jungle. It glances up short-sightedly, snout quivering, but moves on.

I breathe again.

I'm scared I'll find the remains of Sandy's body, a skull or a half chewed leg bone. My legs are shaking so hard I have to sit down. I take out my journal.

After drawing more details on the map—the Buddha and the temple ruins—I move on, leaving a ribbon of thread to mark the temple ruin.

On a small plateau not far from the summit I find a tree

full of ripe rose apples. Gathering as many of the egg-shaped fruit as I can, I eat a few straight away and slip more into the pockets of the rucksack with the figs. (I remember from school that they are lucky fruit, linked in myth with the golden fruit of immortality. Well, I need all the luck I can get.)

There's a steep rock face to climb to what I imagine will be the highest point of the island, so this is probably the best place to get some wood. I've wrapped my sleeping bag around the long bits of wood to hold them together and slung the lot over my shoulder. I find myself enjoying the climbing and my thoughts turn to *Zen and the Art of Motorcycle Maintenance*.

Phaedrus says mountains should be climbed with as little effort as possible, and when you feel like hurrying you should hurry and when you feel winded slow down. Only common sense really. Each footstep should be a unique moment, to be enjoyed and noticed for itself. In other words, live for the moment, not for the attainment of the summit.

I heed his advice, my senses acuter than ever—this rock looks loose.

From this place I can see Dragon Point.

This small-leafed plant lives in this cleft.

Here's where ferns grow.

From this one I can hear gibbons sing.

Every inch I move is mine, my life. I have to make the right decision each time I take a step.

But not all my decisions are right. One small mistake and I lose most of the firewood. It slips out of the makeshift bundle and slides down the rock.

I'm lucky. It could have been me.

I descend once more to gather and repack it. This time I carry it over my shoulders, in the hope that it will be less likely to fall out. As I climb again I recognize the place where I slipped last time and take care not to use that particular foothold. Yes, thank you, Phaedrus.

And finally, I'm here! I've done it! I'm on the top of the island. A pair of three-foot long monitor lizards, shocked by my shout of joy, or maybe they can't stand the smell of me, (and who could blame them?) hurry away. I wonder if I'm the first human to climb to this summit? A pioneer? I should have the Union Jack or better still the flag of St Andrew to plant on top.

I can see all around the island from here. It's made up of lots of small steep hills, like crowded green teeth with a clearing in the middle, where there are no trees, like a huge crater. The one I saw earlier—the salt lick—was much smaller and is over to the north of where I am now. The small mountain I am standing on is much taller than the others. In fact the island looks more oval than circular from this view, with the tail of Dragon Point and the thin white line of our beach far away. I watch the wind's passage through the treetops, like looking over a huge field of swaying green corn. I hear the regular whoosh of waves on the rocky shore, a distant white sound. The rain showers far away on the green and foam-capped sea are like heavy navy blue lace curtains. To the west the wind hurls handfuls of red and green parakeets into the air, like flung confetti. It could almost be paradise. And beyond our island, more islands and islets, too many for me to count.

And not one boat in sight.

I redraw the map, marking *Tiger Cave* and *Butterfly Falls*, the hidden temple, which I rename *Temple of the Golden Buddha*; and this rocky peak—haven't decided a name for it yet. It calls out for something romantic, dramatic. It'll come to me. There is no sign of a plane or helicopter. There's a strong wind blowing but nothing like the hurricane. Large orange clouds hurry across the sky, hounded by darker, puffier, more ominous clouds, like malevolent nuns in billowing habits pursuing fat Buddhist monks.

I need to gather as much firewood as possible, to build the biggest bonfire imaginable, before I attempt to light it. The hunt for wood takes it out of me. My hands are scratched and bleeding from thorns. Wish I had the knife. But the knife is a psychological prop for Jas, in case of unfriendly animals. Jody calls it a Swiss Family Robinson knife.

I'm breaking off a chunk of good dead branch when there's a great sighing and creaking and *crash!*—a huge tree falls and only just misses me. Gibbons screech and howl. Birds rush from the forest into the sky, fruit bats mass like clouds of starlings. My heart thumps against my ribs. The forest seems to be collapsing around me.

I climb the limestone rock-face again and again with my bundle of wood. Harder than it sounds. I wish I had rope. I press as much wood as I can into my rucksack but I can't do it up so I lose bits of wood as I climb.

I rest a moment and take in the 360-degree view once again. It would be wonderful in other circumstances. What am I saying? It is wonderful and I must remember it. Make the most of every step, as I think I remember the writer saying in *Zen and the Art of Motorcycle Maintenance*. This book has turned out to be the most useful thing I packed to come on this trip.

I take out the journal.

I don't want to be an intrepid explorer.
I want to be back in Scotland with my grandparents, a small child again, safe and cared for.

Those weren't the thoughts I'd intended to record, but they were the thoughts that came to me most powerfully as I sat on top of my island.

A memory:

I am never to go out on my own. I can only play indoors or in the dry moat of the lighthouse, sheltered from the raging gales with Leonard, the lighthouse keeper's son, who lets me ride his homemade wooden scooter.

So when I go out with Grandpa, it feels like the best kind of escape. The air rings with the sound of kittiwakes and fulmars wheeling and screaming and the constant wind rustling and blurring the heather. My favourite place is Long Byre, a grassy deep gully where farmers shelter their long-horned cattle in bad weather. We walk through it now and a tiny ball of fluff darts from under my feet—a fledgling skylark—and chirps pitifully from a rock.

'Will its mammy find it, Grandpa?' I am full of remorse and guilt at having frightened the poor wee thing from its nest.

'Aye, Bonnie, it'll signal to its mother and she'll find it, don't you fret.'

Now comes the difficult bit: I must hurry before the sun

disappears. I put a few short twigs in a close criss-cross on a level bit of rock, then I criss-cross broken dead hibiscus twigs on top of them. Then a layer of the driest coconut husk, finishing with a small nest of hairy lichens, which keeps threatening to blow away. Find the broken specs, hold the lens close to the lichens and turn it to catch the sun's rays. Is the sun strong enough this late in the afternoon? Did I blow my chances with all that looking around? A small coin of white heat appears, shimmers and settles. It intensifies. I hold the lens there for several minutes and nothing happens. I see a faint thread of smoke and smell burning. It's happening, fire! Wonderful little flame! A Tinkerbell. I try to remain calm, controlled. I blow gently to spread the flame. The dead twigs burn quickly, too quickly. I heap more on top, then bigger hunks. This is the perfect spot for a fire. No trees close by to catch accidentally. Don't want to send the entire island up in flames, do I?

But no, my fire is dying.

It's gone, my flame has gone. I sob with frustration. I can't even keep a fire going. I blow again. Is it still here? Not a glimmer. Our lifeline —a signal fire.

I can't stop crying. No one will ever find us now. We'll all die, one by one, and no one will ever know. My parents and my grandparents will think I perished at sea, drowned like the boatman. They will for ever think of me as a bloated unrecognizable corpse, broken and chewed by shark and nibbled by fish to a skeleton, for ever drifting over the seabed. There will be no body for them to bury or cremate, no grave or cross for them to grieve over. Nowhere to leave flowers.

Am I feeling sorry for my family, or myself?

I take a deep breath—what would Phaedrus have done? He would work out precisely why the fire had died and do it right the next time, not make the same mistake.

When he took his motorbike engine apart he wrote down every move, so he knew what part went where and how, so he could put it together again. He drew a diagram. That's what I'll do.

What did I do wrong? Too much wood, too quickly? I've killed the fire, like suffocating someone with a pillow. I'll have to start again from scratch.

But the sun won't be there much longer by the look of it. I need to work quickly. I have only a small amount of precious dry lichen and coconut husk left. I don't have time to go back to the forest. I stand and look out at the horizon.

Oh God, there's a boat.

I see a boat, not too far away, heading past the next island. And there's no fire. I've failed. I've failed everyone—poor little Jody and Carly, who have lost their sisters. I've failed Jas. I am as bad as Layla Campbell.

The sun has gone behind a black cloud. I desperately rummage around in my rucksack for more scraps of kindling. Ouch! I've cut my finger. The pain flares. Cut on what? The mirror, it's May's broken mirror. I pull it out gingerly, and wait, hardly breathing, until the sun appears again. Holding the mirror up to the sun I point it in the general direction of the boat, turning my hand up and down slightly. Is it working? Is there a flash of light reflecting towards the boat? Is anyone looking in this direction?

But the little boat is already heading away towards the

setting sun, where the sky is like the marbled endpaper of an old Bible. I collapse in a self-pitying heap and sob. I have failed and night is coming. Shall I stay here on this exposed rock all night on my own as we arranged or try to reach Jas and Jody before the light goes? Oh, Mum, I wish you were here. Or rather, I wish I had never come.

The sudden night is here and I must survive it.

CHAPTER SEVENTEEN

Day 15
Summit of Fire Mountain, interior of Koh Tabu
If I had stayed at the base of the rock I might have been sheltered from the wind but I'm frightened of being trapped by a tiger, for a start. Or the beast that dragged Sandy away—whatever that was. At least here I am safe from predators, I think. Well, I feel safer, anyhow. There's a large slice of yellow moon making an intermittent appearance between huge clouds, and I can see if anything does get anywhere near me.

The torch beam is fainter than it was. I switch it off and try lying down in my sleeping bag, the rucksack as my pillow— that way the wind goes over me instead of through me, but it's a very hard rock. I ache all over. I get up and walk around, back and forth, back and forth to get some feeling in my limbs, slamming my arms against my sides, jumping up and down to keep the blood circulating. I sing loudly, to keep myself company, to keep wild boar away, to scare off tigers. I sing all the old Scottish folk songs Grandma taught me.

> *An' it's Oh! But I'm longing for my ain folk,*
> *Tho' they be but lowly, puir and plain folk.*

I am far beyond the sea, but my heart will ever be
At hame in dear auld Scotland wi' my ain folk.

Jas would laugh if she heard me. She reckons my singing would scare anything away.

Oh ye'll tak' the high road and I'll tak' the low road
And I'll be in Scotland afore ye,
For me and my true love will never meet again
On the bonnie bonnie bank of Loch Lomond.

Oh, dear, that's made me cry. Instead, I fantasize about Lan Kua—about being in his arms. His light brown skin and warm smile, his lips on mine. His spicy breath. The muscles of his arms. Oh, I wish I'd stayed at home.

I force myself to think of Scotland and home, my grandparents' home when I was little: their house is the middle coastguard cottage of the three, with bare floorboards on which I run my Matchbox cars. The wheels make a satisfying whoosh and then a mighty crack as they crash against the skirting boards. The peat fire smokes with a damp earthy fragrance. A home I love.

I peer down into the forest. How are Jas and Jody getting on? I haven't seen a glimmer of their torch. Perhaps they are too well hidden from me. I keep having these visions of a tiger leaping on them, dragging them from the sleeping bag, tearing them limb from limb and devouring them. I briefly flash my torch in their direction but there's no answering beam.

* * *

Another memory:

I wake in the night to the sound of pebbles hitting the window. They have been hurled by the gale and mountainous waves from the rocky beach far below. I call out but no one comes. I scream for an hour or more in the dark, the wind howling in the chimney and rattling the windowpanes. Eventually the neighbour woman comes in to me. I am inconsolable, hysterical. She has to send someone—her husband, I suppose—to fetch my grandparents from the lighthouse.

As the minutes creep by, my thoughts become angry. What is my mum thinking? Does she think I'm dead? Where is she? Where's Daddy? Why haven't they come to look for me? And the parents of all the other girls? If they were alive they would have come, they wouldn't give up, would they? Is Mrs Campbell right? Were the clouds we saw explosions? What was exploding? Cambodia is next door to Thailand. Everyone knows the war has gone there too. Daddy flies there all the time. It's supposed to be secret but we know it's happening. Cambodia's the next killing ground, Daddy said.

When the moon disappears behind cloud and there are no stars to try to identify I stare at the luminous dial of the watch my parents gave me for my fourteenth birthday. It's waterproof. I have snorkelled with it on and it works. What happened to my snorkelling gear? Last time I saw it, it was in a bag in the boat. Did I unload it? Can't remember. We could have caught fish if I had my snorkelling gear.

I remember Dad teaching me to swim. I was four. I wore a snorkel and mask and big blue flippers and he held me under the tummy so I was lying on top of the water, and told me to put my head down so I was looking at the seabed. I was so amazed by what I was seeing—little fish swimming around, the waving sea anemones and coral that looked like pink cabbages, that I didn't realize he had taken his hand away and I was floating on my own. I flapped my big blue feet and moved forward. I was swimming, just like that. He said I wouldn't sink even if I tried to. So I tried and I didn't sink. He was right.

And I remember when I was ten and I had a swimming exam to do and I had a bad cold and Mum didn't want me to do it, Dad said it was my decision. And I did it. And I didn't get pneumonia or bronchitis like Mum thought I would. They've always stood by me whenever I made a decision they weren't too keen on. Like when I chose to come with them to Thailand, leave my school and come with them. I could have stayed with my aunt Beth in Edinburgh, or gone to boarding school, like lots of officers' children, but I wanted to be with them. I couldn't bear the idea of not seeing them for months—we thought it would all be over in months, not years. I'm glad I came with them, even if I've ended up on this island trying to survive. I've lived in the tropics and learned to speak Thai—well, a little. I have met Jas and Lan Kua and eaten wonderful Thai food. There can't be many girls my age who've been marooned on a desert island, discovered a golden Buddha and seen a tiger. I'm probably unique.

* * *

In Borneo I had a pet praying mantis that lived under my mosquito net. It caught any insects that had managed to get through the barrier. He was bright green and watched me as I read in bed. When I spoke to him he moved his articulated long neck and I swear his eyes followed me around the room. Maurice—he was called Maurice, with the accent on the 'ice' like a Frenchman. I didn't tell Mum about him: she would have had him removed. I had two cockroaches living under my bed. (The maid wasn't very good at cleaning.) I fed them breadcrumbs. Naturally, I didn't tell Mum about those either. I was a completely free spirit in Borneo. I never wore shoes. My feet became so thick-skinned I could tread on a thorn and not feel it. I could run on pebbles and it wouldn't hurt. The only problem was scorpions. There were two kinds: blue ones whose sting made you very ill but didn't kill you and black ones, which sunbathed on the wooden walkways of the compound. They could kill you. The local people, the Ibans, showed us how to kill them. The best way was to approach them from the rear so their curved tail was projected forwards and step on them. After Mum came across one on the front step she insisted I wear shoes.

No scorpions here, yet! Instead, ants are biting. How do they survive in this wind? My neck burns from the bites. I scrape the insects from under my sweatshirt collar. Chiggers have burrowed into my crotch and armpits. There's nothing I can do except scratch.

I close my eyes and pull out another Scottish memory:

There are lots of peat bogs, heath and moss, black lochans

where wild ducks paddle and fish, a lighthouse surrounded by a white painted wall. Behind on the hill the low-built little terrace of coastguard cottages, castellated and painted white, huddle from the winds. There are also the remains of buildings that were once radar stations to track U-boats passing through Scapa Flow in the Second World War. These buildings are empty but still frighten me for some reason. I don't like going anywhere near them. In my head they contain something that has the power to destroy my world. The sea almost surrounds us, but the sky is bigger than anything else and is always changing. Huge clouds race from one distant horizon to another. I see in each a lumbering hippopotamus or a castle of glass. My imagination turns thunder-clouds into furious giants. Rainbows are everywhere and nowhere; you cannot catch them even when they end in your back yard. Rain storms move from one part of the coast to another, blanketing the moor, the lighthouse, the grey flat country beyond the headland.

I try to name all the spices and vegetables and other stuff we see at the market in Pattaya: galangal, ginger, coriander, lime leaves, curry leaves, chillies, pepper corns on stalks, tamarind paste, mustard seed, cumin, garlic, cardamom pods, fennel seeds, cloves, mint leaves, star anise, fenugreek, cinnamon sticks, turmeric, mace. I love watching the noodle man make rice sticks, transparent hanks of flat wide noodles.

Shellfish! So many wonderful shellfish: mussels, clams, stalked barnacles, spider crab, green shell crab, limpets, shrimp, tiger prawn, lobster, crawfish . . . uh . . . uh, sea cucumber, seaweed. OK, they aren't shellfish.

I'm *so* hungry. I imagine a big bowl of *phat thai*—flat rice noodles with bean curd, vegetables, egg, peanuts and dried shrimp, with a handful of coriander leaves on top. I can almost smell it. Actually I'd settle for a bowl of plain rice, or better still a big plate of fries with ketchup, or porridge with honey and cream.

What's that? In the dim gleam of the slice of moon that appears briefly from behind a cloud I see two golden eyes, shining and deep, like pools of fire, and there's a smell of something familiar—incense maybe. Then they're gone. Did I see them or imagine them? I'm shaking. They were real. The eyes of a tiger? My own eyes are wide open. I'll never sleep now.

I struggle to see through the gloom and write:

If I survive this, God, I promise I'll be good for ever. I'll never argue with Dad again.

I'm shaking with fear. Why did I ever want to go camping? Why did I come up here on my own? I must be mad. My mouth is dry. I can't swallow, I can't breathe.

Eventually I sit myself up against the rucksack so I'm sort of protected from the worst of the wind, and now that my eyes are accustomed to the dark I can see more or less all around me. I can smell forest smells—earth, leaves, flowers, the faint scent of sea. The forest is not quiet. Perhaps when this is all over, I could come back and study the ecology of the island. I wonder what exams I'd have to take to be able to do something like that? Perhaps I could do it with Jas. She knows so much already.

What am I thinking about? Come back here, with

153

these ants, these chiggers, the mosquitoes! Wild boar and tigers! Oh God, please save me from the tigers! And the snakes.

Another Scottish memory:

I learn to read and write in a schoolhouse that has four to six year olds in the front row where I sit, older children behind, and the fifteen year olds in the back row. We eat bowls of broth at our desks. A peat fire burns in a cast-iron stove in the corner. One morning I jump up and down to get feeling back to my feet and a rubber boot goes flying into the fire.

'I'm telling on ye.'

No need, the stench is appalling. I am carried home through snow as the drifts are too thick for a vehicle.

keep forgetting to breathe. Terror paralyses me.

CHAPTER EIGHTEEN

Day 16?
OK. I haven't been eaten, yet. And I've survived the longest night of my life.

I'm cold and thirsty and ache all over. I'm incredibly itchy. My teeth are coated with what feels like fungus. I can smell myself. When the sun comes up properly I'll thaw out.

The island is blanketed in thick white mist again, apart from the top of my hill. There's no sun. The air smells of spice and seaweed. No birdsong, but I can hear the *hoo-hoo-hoo* of a gibbon choir, far below me in the invisible forest.

Finally the sun breaks through. I jump around to get my legs working again and climb down the hill to find more dry kindling and branch wood. I see a bush with great bunches of crimson berries, but I don't know if they are edible. How did people ever discover what was edible and what poisonous in the old days? Trial and error, I suppose. If you lived it was edible, if you were sick or died no one tried to eat it again. And how did people ever work out what to do with spices like peppercorns, and salt? Potatoes! Who found out that you have to cook them to make them edible? Who invented French fries? The French I suppose.

I lick one of the berries. Yuck, maybe not. (Weren't there poison berries in *Blue Lagoon* called the Never Wake Up berries?) I must remember Dad's edibility test. Don't eat any red plants.

Breadfruit, for example: how did anyone ever find out you have to cook it? Green and knobbly on the outside, rather like unripe enormous lemons. If you roast them in an oven or in the embers of a campfire they sizzle and split to reveal white flesh. The core isn't edible though.

Must concentrate on fire.

This time I have made plaited twine from stripped bark to hold the bundle of wood. I poke at a branch with a long cane to get at a hank of stringy lichen—ideal for tinder—and can't quite reach, so I climb the tree. It's not difficult and I feel warmer already but I am suddenly covered in a sticky orange web and when I look about me to see where its occupant is I come eyeball to eyeball with the biggest spider I've ever seen. It has a spread of about five inches, a long yellow and black body and looks deadly poisonous.

I don't know who is more shocked—spider or me. Me I reckon.

I hurl him from my shoulder quickly before he regains his sense and bites. I hear him plop on the ground. Ugh, big spiders—I hate them. Jas told me once that huntsman spiders' bites have some sort of toxin that liquefies living flesh.

Brown ghosts of cicada casts cling to the tree trunks. There's a termite nest I have to climb around. It's made up of termite crap—digested wood. It would burn well. Perhaps I should hack some off?

But suddenly a cough and sigh comes from below me, then a yelp.

I keep very still, heart pounding, and look down but see nothing. The forest is teeming with life. Big dragon-tail butterflies are flitting in the canopy and in the stripes of sunlight lower in the trees. I reach my lichen and clamber down again, getting yet more sticky web all over me. Spider's webs can be used to cover wounds and aid healing. Why have I thought of that now? If I had thought of it earlier it might have helped Natalie.

There's no sign of whatever yelped.

The sun is higher and stronger now and I make my way back to the mound and my fire site. I'm getting better at climbing, and fire making. This time I get it right. It takes ages to heat the lichen tinder, as I hold the lens close, watching the spot of white heat work its magic. Then when it ignites I place not too much kindling on top of the lichen; a little bit on at a time, patience, then a few dry leaves, a little twig or two, yes, another, more small kindling, get it going, that's it, that's it. In a few minutes I have a real fire going, but it burns fast and I have to keep feeding it. Should have got more wood.

I clamber back down—I'm getting pretty good at this—and have to travel further to find dry timber this time, but with difficulty I drag a long, dead branch back up with me, and break it up onto the fire. The wood crackles and the fragrant smoke grows high to announce our presence on the island. Not so much wind today.

Oh, it's a good fire! Oh, thank you, Hope, for the broken glasses! If only there were a ship or plane to see the smoke!

The euphoria fades as I think about Jas and Jody. Have

157

they left for the beach or is Jody worse and Jas has had to stay with her? My mind races.

I sit by my wonderful fire, feeding it as if it is a hungry dog. It eats fast. The smoke spirals high as the flames die down. I wish I had some food other than rose apples. I have the cramps and have to leave my fire to crap at the base of the rock, where I can cover it up. I feel like a bag lady or a tramp, I'm so dirty. But I can't neglect my baby, my hungry fire. I grab some more dead wood and climb back quick.

The fire is stacked high with plenty of damp stuff and rotten logs. Green wood would be good as it smokes more but I have no axe.

Beetles crawl out from the burning wood and try to escape the fire. Even though I don't mean to I am killing things.

Are Buddhists allowed to light fires if it means insects and grubs will die? The bugs are turned to crisp black beads, rather beautiful, like jet.

I am proud of my fire, it's settling well and will burn for hours with the amount of wood I've placed at its disposal. I say goodbye to it as if it were my friend and had back down the rock for the final time.

I gather more rose apples and eat several for the moisture but almost immediately I am doubled over with more terrible cramps.

My Hansel and Gretel crumbs—the ribbons tied to trees—show me the way.

Ants bite or sting my ankles and I scrape them off with my spear, which I am using as a prod to poke at the undergrowth.

I'm worried about snakes, and everything suddenly looks snake-like: each dangling liana, every root that trips me, and above in the trees, each trembling leaf turns into a serpent in my vivid imagination. It must be tiredness. I've hardly slept for several days and I haven't had enough to eat.

I'd like to be back with my beautiful fire.

Phaedrus worried about the meaning and existence of Quality. He couldn't define it. He wanted students to define it but no one could. He stopped marking exam papers in the university where he worked and upset a lot of people, including his students, who only wanted good grades so they could get well-paid jobs. They didn't care if their work was of Quality or not. In fact, I think that is what finished him off—sent him over the edge and into the pit of insanity. But I'm not sure. When I think about it, Mum is probably very clear about the meaning of Quality.

At the beginning of the book there is a quote:

'And what is good, Phaedrus,
And what is not good—
Need we ask anyone to tell us these things?'

How come Mrs Campbell can't see that what she has become is not good? I don't think she has any Quality at all. She has fallen apart. We haven't been able to depend on her. She may be pretty, when she's showered and shampooed her hair and put on her make-up and everything, but in reality she's ugly, inside she's crap. I don't even blame May and Arlene. They've been led astray. But Mrs Campbell is flaky, unbalanced, loopy. Definitely not Quality.

This is the sixteenth day we've spent here, I think, and

we only had supplies to last three days. But it's no thanks to her that we've survived. It's suddenly terribly important that people understand what's happened on this island. I swing my rucksack from my shoulders and dig around for my journal and pencil. I write in large letters:

Day 16

If anyone gets to read this journal it's because I have failed to survive and get help. I want you to know that you should look into the behaviour of Layla Campbell on this island. Ask any survivors what she did, and what she didn't do. She's partly to blame for the death of Natalie. She had plenty of whisky which could have been used to help disinfect Natalie's injury but she chose to drink it instead. And she's been taking drugs. Encouraging minors to take drugs.

Signed—Bonnie MacDonald, May 1974, Fire Mountain, Koh Tabu

I feel better when I've written it down. I put my journal back in the waterproof holder in my rucksack and climb back down the mountain to find the others.

They've gone. Jess and Jolly have gone. I think this is where I left them. I'm sure it is. It's the only possible place. They must have gone back to the beach. There's no sign of an animal attack. I follow the track we made past the lightning-struck tree, past strange shaped boulders I recognize, through a circular grove where no trees grow but there is a sward of dark ferns. Monkeys and gibbons swoop and swing and call in the high trees. I reach Tiger Cave and need a rest. The hornets are quiet.

I have the runs again. Too many figs and rose apples. I'm shivery and cold, then hot and sweaty. I leave the cave to have a crap, then return, practically crawling, I'm so weak. I want to sleep for ever, but I mustn't give in.

Would I see the tiger if it decided to attack me? Or would it melt into the shadows and suddenly pounce? Perhaps it would get me in my sleep? I know I shouldn't sleep. But I don't think I've ever felt this tired in my life.

The roof of the cave is lit with morning light and as I glance up warily, I see faint ochre images on the rock. When I focus on them properly, they become men running and throwing spears, and the animal they hunt is a big cat with stripes.

A long, lithe tiger.

Wow! Someone must have lived here once, maybe thousands of years ago. Perhaps I'm the first person in the twentieth century to see this cave? I wish I had a camera. I wander further into the cave. There are other paintings, of great dragon-like lizards with flames coming from their mouths, and of small human figures throwing spears at a giant with horns. Like the temple giant, Laksha. And there's a boar hunt. But among the larger images, there are lots of hands, different hands, most smaller than mine with stunted fingers and thumb, but there above the rest, high on the wall I find one huge hand, three times the size of the others. I wander round for ages. Am I the first person— other than the artist—to have seen these drawings?

My mind begins to rattle on. I must remember where this cave is so that when I get back to civilization I can tell someone about what I've found. It might be an important find. I can lead expeditions back to this place. I draw a more detailed map of the location of the cave. A compass would have been useful but I reckon it's more or less in the middle of the island. I also copy the drawings on the cave wall into my journal. The golden Buddha was probably carved long after the cave paintings were finished. The sculpture is far more sophisticated.

While I am sitting quietly drawing and observing, the tiger slinks by, almost hidden in the trees about thirty feet away. She stares at me and I stare back, hypnotized but strangely unafraid. Until I remember that cats count a stare as a sign of aggression. (I think Jas told me that.) So I glance away hoping the cat is not deciding that I'm exactly what she fancies for breakfast.

And I see something orange, like Hope's sweatshirt, disappear into the dark trees. What is it? Did I imagine it? I remember Jody saying she'd seen something similar. This is no imaginary friend. It is real, tall, like Hope, taller. The tiger stops, head turned towards me, grunts like an old dog in her sleep, and walks on away from me.

I haven't breathed since I caught sight of the big cat, and let out a huge sigh of relief. My heart is beating too fast and my hands shaking. I want to laugh. I wish Jas or Hope was here so that I could share the moment with someone. I turn to a fresh page in my journal.

Saw tiger or maybe two! Female, I think.

I drink water and leave the wonderful cave, looking carefully about me all the time.

CHAPTER NINETEEN

It's good to walk. I feel so much stronger, my legs are no longer weak, my cramps have gone. I whistle loudly to frighten away any possible predators—tiger, snake, wild boar—and to comfort myself. The gibbons sing back at me. *Hoo hoo hoooo, hoo, hoo.*

All the rain we've had has brought out fungi. It's suddenly everywhere I look: bullet-shaped fruiting bodies thrust up from the leaf litter and push big leaves and twigs off the ground. The forest floor is covered in a cream brown fungus.

I wonder if it's edible? Better not try it.

I'm still shaking from my tiger encounter, but it's more from excitement than fear. What a story to tell! I imagine a press conference, being interviewed by a handsome reporter. Lots of reporters, from all over the world. Bonnie MacDonald, intrepid explorer and survivor. A TV documentary in which I lead some of the world's most famous naturalists and archaeologists to the cave . . . But from nowhere, a feeling of unease, nausea that has nothing to do with food rises in my stomach. There's such a thing as knowing too much, I think.

My elation now feels embarrassing, shaming. That's not the person I want to be. I wonder how everything could have gone so wrong. It's only days since I was idolizing Mrs Campbell, hoping I'd be something like her when I grow up. Now I question everything about her, I wonder whether anything she's told us is true.

What made Mrs Campbell go wrong? Lose her Quality? If she ever had any. We took her word that she was a survival expert though I can't actually remember when she said that. We believed her when she said she knew the Beatles and the Rolling Stones. That's probably a lie too. She was trying to impress us. She said her husband was a well-known musician. How do we know that was true? Has she ever been truthful?

How do we recognize when a crossroads is reached and we have to make the right decision or ruin our lives for ever by taking the wrong path? Why did we have to come to Thailand? Why did Daddy join the SAS and get deployed to an American unit in the American war against the North Vietnamese? Wh d hu choos g to party ra r har come hi Sh could s ed s all, pre ly, ex ept Sa . could ha op ed he hurric swee ing p Sa ra to have h l ad smashed hat pa m tre

Why d he b tman e? ecause di 't maintain oat engin op er aps he s e Phaedrus's friends, who knew nothing about motors and didn't want to learn? Or was it simply that the extreme weather conditions caused his boat to founder?

But Natalie . . . she was Mrs Campbell's responsibility. Mrs Campbell should have used her alcohol supply to clean the leg wound. She made the wrong decision, a selfish decision. She wanted to escape reality, and drink

164

rice whisky and smoke pot, or whatever it is she was using. She is immoral, or is it amoral? Both probably. Not a good person. Natalie died because of Mrs Campbell's lack of Quality. I feel anger rising in my throat again. At my next stop for water I write.

I hate Layla Campbell. I hope she dies.

How does anyone in power make the right decisions—Quality decisions? When did the US President decide to send military to Vietnam? What was the point of no return? Was it President Nixon's fault or the president before him—Lyndon Johnson?

Maybe I'll study Politics. Become first woman Prime Minister of Great Britain.

We are in a sort of war zone on this island. I am in survival mode; I've become like a wild animal—no time for kindness, empathy, sympathy; I have only to survive.

CHAPTER TWENTY

My mind is so busy with questions that I forget to collect the ribbons and I come to a clearing I don't recognize. Have I gone the wrong way? How could I have taken the wrong path? The strands of towelling are white, easily visible against the dark of the forest.

I go back a little way to find the last ribbon I saw, on the lowest branch of a rattan palm. I'm sure it was here. No. Not here. OK, don't panic, Bonnie, where is it? Where, where, *where*? I turn 360 degrees but can't see a ribbon or any rattan palms. My heart's hammering. I hear my pulse pounding in my head.

I crouch on the leafy floor of the forest o__ my ea_ back.

Calm yourself, Bonnie.

Do some slow breathing.

Think of home, my bed, my blue curtains, their fa__ Mum calling me to supper; Lek's cooking; Daddy coming home looking exhausted. He's probably risking his life every day for us, for me. And I've been horrible to him. He never calls me Puss any more. He hardly talks to me at all. My eyes mist over with tears. What would they do if I were lost for ever? Even if someone comes to rescue us they'll never find *me*, lost in the middle of a forest. I'm like one of the ants scurrying across the leaf litter, living by instinct. If I keep on climbing downhill I'll come to sea level, but it might be on the wrong side of the island.

If only the sun were shining, I'd be able to tell which way was which. The forest is thick here and what sky is visible is dark and dreary with no sign of lightness in it. I look for moss on the tree trunks. I remember learning that it only grows on the north side. Or is it the south side?

Here's a strange rock face I don't remember passing before. In a cleft has been built a little wooden house, like a doll's house. It must be for the forest spirits—*pee bah*. A jasmine wreath shaped like a ring with a tassel lies inside the shrine. The jasmine is so old that it has turned brown and smells of old socks. But who put it there and when? I look around for something to offer the forest spirit. Anything to get me back to the others. Amongst the leaf litter I find an orange leaf covered with a beautiful white fungus, like a miniature coral. I think the spirits will appreciate it. Perhaps they'll feel sorry for me and help.

I have no more water. My feet feel as if they're on fire, my arms and legs are scratched and bleeding. Mosquitoes browse on my arms and legs. The tick and chigger bites itch like mad. My head hurts and behind my eyes blood is pounding. I want to lie down and sleep for ever.

Shadows jump at me. The folk tales Lan Kua tells to amuse and frighten the little ones come back in a rush. They don't scare me at all when he tells them in the light of a bright sunny day, in fact they make me laugh. But now . . . in the dusk . . . scary stories of forest ghosts and spirits swim around my restless brain. There are guardian spirits and tree spirits, so many of them: *Pee-gong goi*—a ghost that jumps around the forest at night on one leg! It sounds so silly, but I'm sure I can hear it stomping around in the dark undergrowth nearby. *Pee Grabang* is a male demon with a long tail. *Pee Pong* prowls during rainfall. *Pee Pret* haunts graveyards and lives on blood and pus. The worst one is *Pee Graseu*—an ugly old woman spirit that eats raw flesh and human faeces, her entrails trailing behind her. Oh yuck, I wish I hadn't remembered that one. Thai folk tales are gruesome. Lan Kua's brothers and little sister must have nightmares all the time.

A terrible wailing makes my blood run cold. The Thais say that a woman who betrayed her lover was turned into a gibbon and forced to roam the forest for ever. That is surely her, full of noisy remorse.

A sudden low *oom*, like a foghorn, stops me in my tracks. I can't see anything. No blazing eyes, no black stripes, no powerful low-hung red body. I take one step forward and there she is. The camouflage is so complete she was invisible. She stands and stares at me from about fifteen feet away. I stare back. She bares her fangs. Terror roots me to the spot.

I bend my knees slowly, pick up a rock, stand and throw the rock at her and scream 'Scram!' As loudly as I can. She bounds off, heavy paws pounding hard, invisible after a second, lost in the trees.

Trembling, I run blindly away from the tiger, through the thorny rattan, climbing figs, bamboos and bushes, tripping over roots and rocks, setting off a ripple of fear through the forest, sending monkeys and gibbons screaming. Toucans clatter, bush turkeys scatter, parrots yell. The entire forest wakes and screams in terror, deafening me.

I'm lost now, with no idea where I am, where I'm going. Struggle through the tangled undergrowth, the thorny creepers, my flesh stuck with spiky rattans. Scramble over slippery roots and leaves, no solid ground beneath my feet and suddenly I'm falling.

Falling.

Tumbling over and over . . . jerk to a sudden stop . . . rucksack straps caught on something. I dangle over a dark deep hole . . . grab at branches, rocks, and lianas to stop myself falling . . . but I can't . . . it's no good . . . I fall out of the straps . . . I'm falling into a deep dark chasm, a rocky ravine . . . mud paints my clothes red, or is it my own blood? I slither . . . hit rocks. My shoulder, legs, hands torn . . . thorns spear my flesh, pain everywhere . . . I fall faster and faster . . . and then . . .

CHAPTER TWENTY-ONE

Shadows . . . sharp stench . . . animal . . . gold . . . black . . .
Black. Moisture at my lips . . . long shadows . . . orange . . .
Pain . . . head . . . arm. Legs, my legs. Green above
me . . . around me. Swinging gently. Black, orange . . . huge
face . . . gentle golden face. The sweet sour smell of rotting
leaves . . . green, cool, water, animal smell, stench. I vomit.
Black . . .

I'm in a boat, swinging on the small waves, sun then shadow
on my face.

An extremely tall skinny man with shaved head wearing
faded orange robes, sits close by. At his feet lies a rer *he*
skinny giant smiles at me, a gentle smile He pours *m*
liquid into my mouth, holding a cloth under my chin to
catch the drips.

I am in a hammock strung between tree trunks. Looking
up into the green canopy of trees I strain to remember my
dream.

'Where am I?' I can't believe I said that. I look around. I put my hands to my temple and find a cloth wrapped around it. The cuts and scratches on my arms and legs have strange green stuff stuck to them and are bandaged with strips of leaves. It smells of fungus and ferns. I drift away . . . water on my lips.

There is a roof of woven leaves above me and the smell of charcoal burning and incense. A spirit house in the form of a miniature temple on bamboo stilts is bedecked with flowers and fruit. There's a sweet smell of jasmine and another strong, pungent reek of wild animal.

I'm not dreaming. As my sight clears I see the tiger rolling on its back like a ginger tabby. The monk unfurls his long snake-like body, he reminds me of Popeye's girlfriend Olive Oyl, and brings me a drink of hot water, with something extra in it, lime-juice and coconut milk I think. It's heavenly. He has a huge head, the monk, misshapen, and his face is sort of twisted, so his fleshy mouth is on one half and his blunt nose and almond eyes on the other. But his gummy smile is friendly. He wears a tiger's claw on a piece of twine around his neck; one shoulder is bare, his orange robe is ragged.

'*Khawp khun*,' I say. 'Thank you.' I try to get out of the hammock but I cannot stand without feeling dizzy. My left leg hurts. He holds me steady until my head clears.

'*Khun phuut phasaa angrit?* Do you speak English?' I have to strain my neck like a baby bird to look up at his face.

He says nothing, shaking his head, and opens his drooling mouth, pointing inside. He seems to have no tongue or teeth.

The tiger pushes itself up onto its legs and comes towards us. I freeze. The great beast comes to my side and rubs itself against my legs, nearly pushing me over, and ambles away. The monk laughs and strokes the tiger's head. I swear it's purring.

My head feels awful and my brain is reeling. The monk, who must be seven feet tall, though he is so skinny his bones jut from his flesh, takes my hand and leads me to the tiger's side. Squatting, he indicates that I should sit also and stroke the massive beast. The fur is hot, the panting flanks are real, not imaginary. This big cat is tame. We haven't been attacked because she isn't afraid of Man. She hasn't been hunted. She only knows this gentle giant. This is some sort of Eden. I stay whispering to the tiger for an age. She seems curious about me, nosing my hands, snuffing at me like a big dog. She sneezes. The monk is very amused. Who is he? How did he come to be here? I am dizzy and get back into the hammock. I watch the monk as he lifts something which has been cooked on a rack surrounded by hot stones and buried in an oven not unlike the charcoal burner's fire in our compound. It's a sweet-smelling root, and it's delicious, like sugar, carrot, and potato all in one. He passes me a sweet drink, which I think of as tiger's milk, but of course it can't be.

I drift into semi-consciousness, waking myself with sudden shouts. He presses more of the fruity drink to my lips. I am feverish, but aware always of the monk's quiet presence, his long fingers on my burning forehead, the dressings on my cuts changed. The tiger lies panting in the shade, long whiskers twitching, long tongue lolling . . . curved yellow fangs.

* * *

My mother and father run towards me, flames engulf them.

I no longer know what is real, what is unreal. Is the tiger really licking my hand? I smell fur, like burnt toffee.

I wake to darkness, but the monk is there still, smiling his crooked smile. I have no idea how long I have been here but at least my injuries are not terrible: no broken bones, though I hurt all over.

A huge tusked boar is charging at me, my legs won't move. It screams, or I do.

My full bladder wakes me. I keep saying 'pee-pee, pee-pee', and he seems to understand, smiling widely and nodding. He helps me to my feet, takes me to a perfectly decent latrine at the edge of his camp and turns his back. I crouch and relieve myself and he takes me back to my swinging bed. Have I taken his bed from him? Where is he sleeping? I could sleep for ever.

Explosions, flames, the stench of burning oil. A tree falling towards me. I am paralysed. A cock crows.

173

* * *

My rucksack is by my side. How did it get there? Thought I'd lost it for ever, stuck on a branch in a crevice.

Today—whatever day it might be—I feel a little better. Still shaky and weak, but the hammer in my head has stopped and I am actually hungry. When the gentle monk accompanies me to the latrine I can actually walk without his help. Well, nearly.

The tiger comes and goes silently. Sometimes her cheeks and throat are bloody. She spends ages cleaning herself, just like a domestic cat—her long rasping tongue—the yellow fangs. She lies on her back, her nipples pink on the honey coloured fur. The monk has a small woven bamboo fenced yard with three black hens and a fine cockerel, whose red comb quivers and shakes as he struts.

I am being fattened with eggs. They taste like nectar. No more fever. My leg injury still weeps with yellow pus but the swelling is going. The man who saved my life dresses the various cuts all over me with a mess of chewed leaves wrapped with whole leaves and tied with shredded bark.

I have no idea how long I have been here. Jas and the others must wonder what has happened to me. Oh, God, what if someone has rescued them and left me here? My thoughts crash around. They have no place in this peaceful heaven.

Sunshine spatters the clearing beyond the cave mouth. The monk silently offers me spongy nut from a sprouting coconut for my breakfast.

174

My rucksack was battered and torn in the fall but my journal is safe.

I still have a pencil, and I have tried to record what I remember of what's happened since I left Fire Mountain.

I am becoming restless. I need to move on, and I see that he understands this.

I wish I had something to give the monk, a thank you present. I haven't really anything that would be of use to him. But I have been drawing sketches of the tiger in my journal; I tear out a page, which he accepts with a large wet smile.

He leads me to a limestone cave. He sleeps here on a small platform packed with dry grass, and on the rock wall I see a mural of giant handprints. He smiles and places his hand onto the wall and I see that it's *his* huge hands that are multiplied across the rock. It's like a schoolroom wall of kids' finger-paint prints, or a surreal design for wallpaper, each pinky touching the one of the other hand, and the thumbs touching—a repeated pattern. But instead of a community of friends' or of family hands reaching out to be close to each other, the monk has only himself. There is a sort of red paste in a gourd bowl on the floor of the cave. He mimes to me to put my hands in the bowl and then place them on the cave wall. I make my mark on his cave of hands, my small hands low down, his big signature above.

He gives me more water in a flask, fills a sack with pawpaw, limes, mangosteen, and cooked eggs, and taking me by the hand again leads me through steaming forest. It's time for me to leave. The tiger follows, swaying silently. Toucans honk noisily above, bush turkeys are creeping and scraping through the leaf litter.

The path suddenly opens up to pines and banana trees

and elephant grass, taller than me, taller than the monk. The tiger leaps ahead. Gibbons *hoo hoo* in alarm. And here is our destination—a lake! I think this must be the crater I saw from the summit. The tiger bounds heavily to the edge, turns away from the water and plunges in backwards as if she doesn't want to wet her whiskers. We squat, the monk and I, at the edge of the lily covered water. Egrets lift together from the water in a white flutter like torn paper and pass over our heads. He smiles always, at me, at the tiger, at the birds. Then he slips into the shallows and beckons me. I stand at the edge, peering into the dark water, the ripples distorting the trees' reflection. I'm dizzy. I crouch, and turn into the water, much as the tiger did, backwards, immersing myself slowly. The water is cool on my hot skin, like clean cotton sheets. I float on my back, calm and almost pain-free, content simply to lie, looking at the dark towering clouds, happy.

However he came to be here, cut off from society, he is happy. I wonder if he carried the cub here, or was she here before him? I'll never know. He lives in perfect harmony with his big cat, like a saint or a spirit.

Sounds are muted in the cotton-wool-like warmth of the water. The cat swims silently. Large butterflies flap lazily down to sip from the surface. Invisible parakeets squabble in the trees. Above the water is a haze of mosquitoes; dragonflies hover and sip. The tiger rises from the water, dripping gold. I feel clean, safe, entranced. She shakes herself, scattering diamonds from her darkened fur.

We follow a narrow path up and down and around the green hills, the tiger ahead, then the monk, with me at the rear.

I am not as strong as I thought. I crouch to get my breath. My head spins. A sudden loud snort and angry squeal and a huge-tusked boar breaks through the forest onto the trail and straight at me. In terror I instinctively throw myself out of the way.

A golden belly above me, like a blinding flash of sun.

The wild boar screams as the tiger's jaws close. I'm shaking and sobbing, laughing and trembling. The monk smiles broadly and claps his hands. He bends to reach me and lifts me up away from the tiger and her bloody victim.

I am half fainting and dizzy still. He carries me through dark forest, trees pushing in at us from all sides until we come to more open savannah, where he lets me stand. I am rested now and the trembling has stopped.

We continue our trek, without the tiger, who is presumably enjoying her feast.

The monk does not hurry me, but I am aware that he wants me to go now, back to my world, leaving him to his. His long hand sits on my head. He puts a finger first to his chest, then points towards me and then to his destroyed mouth to urge me to be quiet. His message couldn't be clearer. He removes the string with the tiger claw from around his neck and places it over my head. Then he hands me the sack of fruit and waves me on alone, pointing in the direction I must go, and smiling, puts his hands together in a prayer and bows.

I do the same to him.

When I raise my eyes he is gone.

* * *

Above the thumping of my heart and head I hear a honking noise, like the sound of wild geese in Scotland. No, it's the conch. Someone is blowing the conch.

It must be Hope. I follow the sound downhill. Please blow it again, Hope. Yes, I must be going towards the beach, even though there are no markers. I push my way through, desperate to reach the beach and friends. I only hope that Jas and Jody are safe. Please God . . .

There is something familiar hanging in a bush of red flowers. Mrs Campbell's guitar. I reach for it, ignoring the thorns. It's broken of course; holed and smashed, all but one of the strings twisted and snapped in two. Then I smell seaweed.

The forest thins and earth turns to sand. I recognize familiar rocks and trees. Feathered crowns of stooping palms hiss and dip in the strong breeze. The relief of coming at last to the beach: it's almost like coming home.

CHAPTER TWENTY-TWO

I don't believe it: they've made a raft. Without me they've built a raft. Hope is hammering away at something, and jumps when I appear.

'Oh hi, Bonnie, you're back.'

I'm astonished.

'Is that all you have to say?'

'Oh, sorry. What have you done to your head? Do you know your leg's bleeding?'

'Hope, this is . . . it looks like a real raft. Does it float?'

'Sure it floats. I think. Built it all on my own.' Hope looks different, sounds different.

'Is Jas here?' I collapse onto the sand.

Jas runs towards me on cue. I don't recognize her at first—she's so skinny. I somehow thought she'd look like she did when we set out on the camping trip. But she's lost her glow, her healthy plumpness.

'Bonnie, oh Bonnie, are you OK? Where have you been? It's been three days. Thank goodness you're safe. We saw the smoke on the mountain. What's happened to your head? And your leg? Where's that orange bandage from? What's that around your neck?' She's holding my shoulders, shaking me with every question.

'How's Jody?'

'Oh, Jody's fine. No problem, apart from chiggers in her feet. I tried to dig them out, but there's infection. Thought I better get her back here though as we arranged. Followed the stream. It was much easier going. We got back really quickly.'

'You didn't meet up with anything on the way?'

'Like what?'

'Tiger? Wild boar?'

'No, we were fine.'

'You wouldn't believe the adventures I've had. I was—'

Hope interrupts our reunion. 'Excuse me, guys. Forget your travellers' tales. What about my raft?'

'Yeah, it's fantastic, Hope.' I sit on the edge and test its strength. It's about fourteen feet long, made of seven logs strapped together, with five cross pieces to strengthen it. Only Hope is strong enough to have manhandled the logs to the beach.

'How did you manage to cut the wood?'

'With difficulty and brute strength. And with the help of your Swiss army knife. Jas lent it to me.' She sounds proud of herself. And the stutter—it's gone.

'To tell the truth, most of the trunks were already broken off by the storm.'

'What did you use to bind the logs together?'

'Balsam wood bark. It's brilliant. You strip it off, see . . . '

'But how did you know what a balsam tree looks like?'

'I dunno, I just knew. I build model planes.'

'How come you didn't tell us you could build things?'

'You never asked. I'm only the babysitter.'

'Where did you get that orange bandana, Bonnie? And

180

what's wrapped round your arms?' Carly and Jody join us, drawn by the conch. 'You're all cut and bruised. Your leg's bleeding. What's that around your neck? Where've you been?'

'It's a tiger claw, Jody. I . . . I found it . . . with the cloth. I fell and banged my head. I . . . and a wild boar charged me, but I escaped . . . '

'Oh yeah? Pull the other one,' says Jas.

The juniors are bored by talk and wander back to sand-castle building.

'Never mind that now. Come to the camp and I'll bathe your leg. It looks sore.'

'Oh Jas, it's so good to be back. I was lost.'

'You're safe now.'

'No boat?'

'No boat.'

I find my cheeks are wet. So much for my Quality fire.

'We need to protect ourselves from big boars, Jas.'

'Like May and Arlene, you mean?' Jas says. I don't laugh.

'Did I mention I saw a golden Buddha? And . . . and there's a lake in the middle of the island—a big lake.'

'A lake? Volcanic crater?'

'Oh, I forgot these.' I hand over the sack of fruit and cooked eggs to Jas, who acts as if I have given her a triple strawberry ice-cream sundae with chocolate sauce and sprinkled almonds.

'But what . . . ? How did you . . . ?'

'Jas, don't ask. Please, don't ask. I can't tell you.'

'OK, OK. But . . . '

'No, I'm not telling you anything more. I fell, that's all, and I did survive a wild boar charge. That's it, that's all you're going to get.'

CHAPTER TWENTY-THREE

Koh Tabu, May, or maybe June 1974.
I have no idea what day it is or how long we've been here. Jas
says 18 days, Hope says 20.

Fantastic scabs are forming all the way up my left leg and
on both elbows. I have a great scar on my temple apparently—
shaped like a diamond. Bruises of all shades of blue, green, and
yellow, decorate my body and limbs like camouflage paint on a
plane.

No one's seen any planes or boats near the island lately and
there have been only rare sightings of the Barbie Babes and
Loopy Layla.

We work—Hope, Jas, Carly, Jody, and I—to build a more
secure enclosure of sharpened bamboo canes against the
threat of rampaging wild boar. We trek together into the
forest to collect the canes, making a lot of noise, banging
tin cans together, armed with spears, shouting and singing,
hoping the nasty creatures will run *away* from us, not at us.
The gibbons complain loudly, screaming at us from high
branches.

Hope is stronger than the rest of us. She's lost weight, but
she's more muscular.

She's wearing the broken glasses, the blind eye covered

with the boatman's black eye-patch. Her head is covered by Carly's red bandana, pirate-like. Jody calls her Cap'n Hope. Hope lives up to the image, calling us 'me hearties'. She chops the long thick bamboo canes off at the base with the cork handled curved knife and the rest of us carry the bundles of canes between us from the forest back to the beach.

'Black Cave is the best camp,' says Jas. 'We can get a good view of anything that's coming towards us.'

'Yeah, we can see a long way,' says Hope. 'But it's too small a space.'

I'm not used to Hope stating her case.

'We can't build a fence round the cave. Where could we stick the poles? There's only rock,' I point out. So in the end I win the argument and we decide to use the natural shelter of the banyan tree, much to the disgust of Jody and Carly who consider it their own special private camp, and the superstitious Jas, who is convinced that it is bad luck to sleep under it.

'Oh come on, Jas,' I say, 'we are hardly likely to have more bad luck than we have had already.'

'But in the *Jataka* tales, in the story of *Satyavan and Savitri*, Satyavan lost his life beneath the branches of a banyan. All sorts of spirits and ghosts live in the branches of the banyan. *Kinnaras*, half-human, half-animal. That's why Thais don't like to sleep under them.'

'Ghosts?'

'Take no notice of her, Jody. It's only a story, like Santa Claus.'

'Santa? What do you mean?' she whines. '*He's* not a story.'

Oh God!

* * *

Having transferred practically the entire island plantation of bamboo canes to the top of the beach Hope and I cut the tops off at an acute angle, to make sharp points. Pushing the canes into the sand is harder than it sounds. We can't hammer them in, as there is no flat top to the canes any more. Instead we dig deep holes for each pole and then pile the sand around the upright cane and stamp it down, like planting a sapling tree. Most of them collapse as soon as we let go and we have to start again, digging deeper with whatever we have to hand, the shovel, coconut shells, driftwood, brute strength. It's exhausting work but we are getting there. Slowly the enclosure grows around the main tree trunk, although the dozens of secondary trunks make it difficult. After a whole day of cutting, carrying and digging we have the semblance of a safe encampment, a corral.

Between each vertical we pack in bundles of branches and palm leaves to fill the gaps. No boar will break through that.

There's plenty of wood damaged by the storm for the fire. But there hasn't been a chance of using Hope's glasses to start a fire as the weather is awful. Even when it isn't actually raining it looks as if it will at any moment. Clouds rumble threateningly and the sky is dark purple-green and black like a bad bruise. The wind whines and moans in the remaining palms. We're getting used to the way the fine sand crusts our lips and eyes.

One good thing comes from our search for bamboo. We come across several papaya trees that had obviously come down in the storm. The fallen fruit smells like perfumed melon. Papaya will make a change from coconut anyway. We still have a few mangosteen. The delicious eggs have been eaten.

Inside the barricade we do feel safer. It's rather maze-like with the supporting root branches forming tunnels. We drape the sail over the branches to make it a bit more rainproof, but then realize that we would probably do better to keep the sail for the raft. So we make a thatched roof, weaving palm leaves together and knitting ferns and large leaves into it. It takes an age and our hands are torn and sore. We have removed the corrugated bamboo pole roofing from the cave extension and used it here instead. Our narrow gate is a well-camouflaged brush and palm-leaf section between two sharpened bamboos. We are inside a cage and the wild boar are on the outside.

Night—by the campfire

It occurs to me that what the boatman said about the island being taboo to locals (and he said something about a Yaksha) might have all come from someone seeing the seven foot monk with the strange-shaped head and face, and thinking he was a temple giant, or a forest spirit. And I think of something Dad said about Buddhist monks being murdered in Cambodia. Maybe he's escaped from there. He probably has got a boat, though I didn't see one on the lake. We could use it to get home. I could go back and find him. I promised him I would keep silent. No one must know about him. No one.

We haven't seen anything of Loopy Layla and her cohorts, her goons—the Barbie Babes. What can she be thinking of? If we ever get out of here she'll be in so much trouble. I just feel so angry. I want to hurt her.

Jas and I walk up the beach to the cave to see if Mrs Campbell and the Barbie Babes are there. They aren't; though there are signs that they still sleep there—stinking sleeping bags and half full water bottles.

We climb the rocks of Dragon Point and over to the other beach beyond and go a little way into the forest.

'What's that hanging in the palm tree?' Jas asks me.

I can't believe my eyes. 'Hooch! She's fermenting coconut milk.'

'How do you know that, Bonnie?'

'I've seen it before, in Borneo.'

Layla Campbell is unbelievable! The evidence is hanging in a small palm tree: a young green coconut with an incision in the base. Under it hangs a water bottle catching the drips. The resulting liquid will be highly alcoholic. Didn't Mum tell me once it could blind you?

'What a shame she doesn't put as much effort into looking after us!' I spit out the words.

'What are those things on the sand?'

May's hair curlers litter the sand like strange sea creatures.

We call but they aren't to be seen.

'It would have been good to sort things out with her and the Barbie Babes before we try out the raft,' says Jas. 'She should be with the juniors.'

'Some hopes!' I retort and kick at the undergrowth. I can't believe I used to think so much of her. I'm almost as angry at myself as I am with her.

We have to make a decision about the raft.

'How many will it carry, do you think?'

'Let's try, shall we? I've been dying to try it out.'

First we heave two fallen palm tree trunks to where the raft is on the sand. Using them as wheels we lift the raft onto them and Jas, Hope, and I, with Carly and Jody helping, drag and push it into the water of the fishing pool. Hope and I clamber onto it. It feels stable and there's plenty of room for more people.

'How do we steer it, or propel it?' I ask.

'Haven't got round to that yet,' says Hope. 'We've been too busy with the camp fencing.'

'Yeah, well, it's important, keeping us safe from wild boar.'

'Yeah, OK, Bonnie, keep your hair on. Got any suggestions?'

I think. My grandpa uses an oar at the stern of their rowing boat to scull the craft along. It acts as rudder and paddle.

'Give me time,' I say.

'It's great, Hope, just amazing,' calls Jas from the beach. We drift around, pushed and pulled by the wind, and gaze into the shallows of the pool. Orange and white striped clown fish dart into and out of the tendrils of sea anemones and slender blue fish quiver in the fronds of fan-like pink coral. A large shell-dwelling creature propels itself along by a strange muscular foot. Sea cucumbers are like giant slugs. Transparent shrimp jump backwards. I could stay for ever gazing into this strange, quiet world.

I wonder if the creatures have a language, make sounds inaudible to us? Do they gossip and chatter and tell each other of danger? I bet they do. All creatures seem to have their own conversations, even silent highland cattle in a field, nodding and shaking their shaggy heads at each other. I wish suddenly for Scotland, cool clean air, the scent of heather, gorse, and peat and the clean cold sea smell of the Atlantic.

'I'm coming. I want to get on,' shouts Jody.

'Come on then,' Hope calls to them.

The others splash out to us and clamber on. With all of us aboard it sinks a little, the deck submerged just under the surface, but it still floats.

'Help, it's sinking.' Jody jumps off and wades ashore, throwing these words over her shoulder—'You could use the shovel as an oar.'

'Yes, of course, brilliant, Jody.' Jody glows under the admiring words from Jas.

Hope looks happier than I've ever seen her. Who would have thought she could be so enterprising? I'm sorry I pooh-poohed her idea before. She has hidden depths, Hope. I must remember to tell her.

Whispering about it later with Jas, when we settle down for the night, she says Hope has probably lost her stutter because she has gained faith in herself. She feels at last that she has some control over her life. OK, I can understand that. I just hope that when she returns to her family her father doesn't belittle her and make her life miserable again.

My description of the cave drawings intrigues Jas. She wants to see them too.

Lying in the dark, the familiar sound of crashing waves and buffeting wind keeps me awake. Not wanting to turn on a torch to write in my journal and wake Jas, I make a mental list of things to do:

1. Make a rudder. How? Possibly with the shovel, though I'm not sure how to fix it.
2. We need to load our raft with plenty of fresh water.
3. Rig a sail.
4. Find very long poles to punt ourselves along in shallow water.
5. Food. We need to collect coconuts and whatever fresh fruit we can find. Water bottles.
6. Fishing line.
7. Salt, hats, clothes to protect us from sun—if we ever see it again.
8. Decide who is going, who is staying.

CHAPTER TWENTY-FOUR

Koh Tabu, Gulf of Thailand, May or June 1974
Today I, Bonnie MacDonald, am going to save us all—I
hope. I feel optimistic. I think we can do this—sail to an
inhabited island to get help. Or find someone on a fishing
boat who can help. Maybe this will be the last of my journal
entries?

In the morning we gather on the beach, all of us apart from
the Barbie Babes and Loopy Layla, who are still missing,
presumed drunk and/or stoned. First we have the naming
of the raft: the juniors have written HOPE in May's lipstick
on the sail.

'Where did you get the lipstick?' Jas asks Jody.

'Er . . . can't remember. Found it.'

'To a safe voyage and deliverance from this island,' I say.

We solemnly clink coconut shells together and drink a
toast.

'I name this ship HOPE,' Jas announces. 'God speed to
her and all who sail in her.'

Hope can't stop smiling. Then there's silence as we all
think about what happened and what the future holds. The
juniors look frightened.

'Mrs Campbell should be here,' says Jas, quietly.

'Yeah, well, some hopes,' I say.

'Having a divided party isn't good. It's like two enemy tribes. We should all be pulling together.' Jas looks sad.

'Never mind about them. Let's decide about the crew,' I say.

'Anyhow, I'm not going on that thing,' says Jody. She looks as though she might cry.

'We can't all go,' I say.

'I hear what you're saying,' says Hope.

'No, not you, Hope. You have to go, it's your raft,' says Jas.

'I don't mind staying.'

'No, I'll stay.' Jas is her usual self-sacrificing self. It doesn't occur to *me* for a moment to offer to stay behind.

'You sure?' says Hope.

She shrugs. 'Of course. Can't leave the juniors to look after themselves. Anyway, it'll go faster if there are only two of you. And you're the strongest.'

[several lines obscured]
There's a strong onshore wind blowing, but they aren't being blown away. Instead, there are building, [...] and dark thunder rumbles all around [...] and [...] grey [...] on there are flashes of sheet lightning.

'Shouldn't we wait until the weather improves before we set off?' Hope is looking less upbeat about our voyage.

'No, it might never improve.' I am eager to get started.

'But it hasn't been tested, we don't know if it's seaworthy.'

'Hope, it's wonderful. It floats. We'll be fine. We can't put it off. We need to get help *now*. *Who dares wins!*'

192

'Whadyamean?'

'It's the SAS motto.'

'What's that got to do with anything?'

'My dad's SAS. It means you have to be brave to achieve anything.'

'OK, OK.' She capitulates.

I'm beginning to have my doubts about her commitment.

'The Amelia Earhart Cadet motto—*Try Your Best*—is sort of puny compared to the SAS one,' I say, clapping her on the back.

We make sure the raft is pulled up above the tide line while we go off to collect provisions for the voyage, Jas holding onto my arm.

'Why not wait a while, Bonz?'

'No, we need to get help now.' I give her the waterproof holder with my tattered journal in. 'Jas, you promise not to read my journal?'

'Sure, I promise. What do you think I am?'

'If anything happens to me, you can.'

'Bonnie, you'll be fine. I'll look after it.' She plants a kiss on my head.

'Hide it from the others.'

'Yeah, yeah.'

We have spent half a day fixing up the raft. We've rigged a simple sort of sail using the canvas from the boatman's wreck. For a rudder we use the juniors' seesaw: a long plank of barnacle-covered wood, very basic, but it's all we have. I've shaved it with the wood-saw of my army knife so it is paddle shaped, more or less, and I've mounted it at one end of the raft. It won't stand much violent shifting, but if we are lucky and careful . . . And we have a couple of punting poles made from thick branches of an unidentified tree that was pushed over by the storm. We also have the shovel to use as an oar.

'Where will you go?' Jody asks me.

If we can get to the next island, which is about a mile away, I guess, we'll be more visible to passing boats or planes. We have to try something anyway. Ko Chang, the inhabited one, is too far away.

At high tide Hope, Jas, and the juniors push us off. I am on the raft, in charge of the rudder.

'See you later, alligator.'

'In a while, crocodile,' they all shout from the shore. Hope wades after me and climbs on board when we are beyond the breaking surf. We have several false starts. The raft rises, plunges and turns back on itself the first couple

of tim . . . t re t he . . . les
ecom . . . n re a w . . . cal
e fort . . . a a a an . . . us
c ut, tl . . . e r j m p . . . the
s allo . . . t l 7 p . . . ves
a d ac . . . v ds e .

At f . . . p le e . . .

Hope is in charge of the sail and I look after the rudder, for now, but we've agreed to take over from each other when we need to.

'Wow,' Hope grins at me, 'we are actually moving in more or less the right direction.'

On the beach, waving and getting smaller and smaller, are Jas, Jody, and Carly.

'I hope they'll be OK,' says Hope as she waves back with one hand and grips our sail with the other. I want to reassure her but I can't so I smile and point towards an island in the distance.

'Thataway, Cap'n. We have a long way to go.'

We are nearing the reef and the water is becoming more turbulent as we head for the open sea. We have to somehow manoeuvre the unwieldy raft through the gap in the reef. I thought the high tide would cover the rocks but it hasn't.

Suddenly I realize we aren't going to make it and a massive blow on the rudder knocks me over.

'Help . . . Hope!' I scream. 'The rudder! Can't hold it. *Help!* Now!'

Too late, I feel the rudder snap and what remains is swept from my hands as if it's alive.

'Poles, the poles . . . ' Hope is pushing with all her might, balancing herself on her knees. Yes, it's working. We use the poles to keep the raft from hitting the reef but we're going round in circles. I don't know whether to laugh or cry. Hope paddles furiously with the spade but the raft is completely out of our control, swept in a downward spiral . . .

'Abandon ship! Jump!' My words are whisked away in the yell of pounding surf as I jump away from the reef into the boiling sea. Hope follows.

I strike out for the beach, swimming strongly to escape the turbulence and pull of the waters rushing through the exposed coral. I'm a good swimmer. I can reach the shore. Hope is fine; her crawl's almost as strong as mine. It could be even stronger. Looking over my shoulder I see the raft rise from the swell then, lifted, dropped, and smashed as if a clenched fist has broken a bundle of twigs and thrown them into the air.

I lose sight of the beach. I'm plunged into the valleys of the waves. This is nothing like swimming in a pool. I swallow water and choke. Is Hope still there? I see her, but she has drifted away from me and is swimming parallel to the beach instead of towards it. For a moment I think she knows what she's doing, but then I realize—of course, her eyes! She can't see where she's headed.

'Hope, Hope! This way . . . *Hope!*' Scream of sea and wind drowns my calls, and I can't catch my breath to force more noise from my lungs. I try to swim towards her but I can't see beyond the hills and troughs of waves.

My mind is full of shark. I have a brief image of Dad, laughing at me. 'You and your imagination, Bonnie.' But the fear is terribly real. At that very instant I think I see a black fin away in Hope's direction. I tread water, trying to see Hope, trying to see the fin. Nothing. I imagined it. Then I see an arm lifted from the water—in greeting or in desperation? A thin high scream reaches me. A seabird? Is it Hope? Maybe *I* screamed?

I strike out again, swim for my life now, towards the beach, move faster than I ever move in swimming tournaments; don't look left or right, simply keep my eye on the beach ahead. Strike out for the beach, for safety.

As I near the surf breaking on the shore I hear the other girls calling, glance them leaping up and down on the beach, waving at me, encouraging me. It's like the finish of a race, my family and friends cheering me on. I'm the winner. Jas wades out and half drags, half hinders me as I get there, falling into the waves with me. She's sobbing.

'Oh, Bonnie. We saw it. We saw the raft wrecked.'

I cough and splutter. 'Hope?'

'No!'

We stare out at the tumbling white water, and at the ranks of mountainous waves in the lagoon. She's not to be seen.

'What's that?' Jas points at a black object in the distance over towards the gap in the reef, where we lost our raft. It was the unmistakable, dread shape, the black triangle.

We never see Hope again.

CHAPTER TWENTY-fivE

We're holding each other, Jody, Carly, Jas, and me, holding each other tight and crying. Mrs Campbell, May, and Arlene come staggering towards us from the direction of Black Cave. They are thin and haggard, with dark bags under their eyes, their hair wild and tangled, greasy and flattened. Mrs Campbell is practically unrecognizable.

'We saw,' said Mrs Campbell. 'It was terrible. We saw the raft go down.' Her mouth twitches and she puts a hand to her wrecked hair.

'Did you see what happened to Hope?'

'No, I lost sight of her.'

'She just sank,' said Arlene.

'She was heading in totally the wrong direction,' May smirked.

'She couldn't see,' I scream. 'She couldn't see where she was going.'

'I'm sorry,' said Mrs Campbell.

What is she sorry about? That she has been worse than useless; a total waste of time? That she takes mind-bending drugs? That she gave May and Arlene drugs? That she was responsible for Natalie's death? Or that Hope has died? I turn from her and walk away from everybody, along the thin strand of sand, only wanting to be alone. My nose streams with salt water. I cough and spit up phlegm and find I am vomiting. I fall to my knees and then my belly, holding onto the sand as if it is solid ground. Jas runs to me and holds my shaking shoulders but I push her away.

'Leave me, leave me. Go away!'

She shoves the sand with one foot, but says nothing.

The dizziness goes eventually, and the nausea, but I am left weak and shivering. Not only have we lost Hope, we've lost all means of making fire—Hope's broken glasses.

The wind has dropped. My mind crackles with furious thoughts. If only we had waited, we could have steered through the reef. If only . . . if only . . .

Thunder cracks loudly overhead followed by a blinding flash, and a torrent of rain falls from the low sky. It hurts. The huge drops are like small opaque white cannon balls and they leave craters in the sand like those photographs of the surface of the moon. I turn and run with the others to the meagre shelter of our enclosure. Our roof is useless; we are as wet as if there were no thatch. I can almost hear the rain spirits—*pee pah*—laughing at us, glad we are marooned on this island.

Later, much later, I retrieve my journal from Jas and start writing:

The boatman was right: we should never have set foot here. It is a terrible place; it will kill us all. We are like the people at the party in a foreign movie I saw with Mum. We cannot

*leave, must stay here for ever and live like animals, or go
mad, and die.*

It's my fault. I should have listened to Hope.

I am responsible for her death.

CHAPTER TWENTY-SIX

High in the sky several large birds circle. We hear them cry, a deep mew, like a trapped cat, a sound that makes my heart stop.

'They're vultures, aren't they, vultures waiting for us to die?' says Arlene tearfully. May has nothing to say, for once.

'Kites, I think, not vultures,' says Jas. 'Maybe Brahmini kites. Red on the back, white underneath.'

I sit saying nothing. I have said nothing since I returned to the shelter, and the others say nothing to me. It's as if I'm a stranger. Briefly, I wonder how Jas can bring herself to teach us anything new . . . but as always I listen to what she says. And after a moment's silence, I break mine.

'Kites! A kite!' I shout, surprising even myself. 'That's the answer—a kite.' I twist off my bottom onto my knees, facing them all. 'If we can't get smoke we can have a kite.' My words tumble out of my mouth. 'Wind we certainly do have. It's what we have most of, apart from seawater and rain. If we could make a high-flying kite someone would see it and know there is someone on this island. They would know where to find us. I've seen Lan Kua make kites for his little brothers and sisters . . . And we've flown them often enough . . . ' I stop, suddenly breathless.

I have to think carefully. If I can only remember how to do it . . .

I draw a simple kite shape in my journal, mark the components like Phaedrus did with his motorcycle, and show the others.

We gather our lightweight clothes together, whatever we can find, the two red neckerchiefs, the orange rag from the monk. Using two thin bamboos I make an A-frame, tied in the middle with the fishing line, very basic but workable. I make notches at the ends of each stick and cut a piece of string long enough to stretch all the way around the kite frame. I make a loop in the top notch and fasten it by wrapping the string around the bamboo stick. Then I stretch the string through the notch at one end of the cross-piece, and make another loop at the bottom. Next I stretch the string through the notch at the other end of the cross-piece. I finish by wrapping the string a few times around the top of the stick and cut off the excess string. It looks great, taut and square and the bamboo sticks are not bent, not under stress.

Now I position one of the neckerchiefs to fit the frame with a bit of order, a margin. It's difficult cutting through fine cotton with a knife. Then I remember there's a tiny pair of scissors in my knife. I get Jody and Jas to stretch the fabric between them so it's taut before I begin to cut it.

'We haven't got any glue. How are you going to stick the material to the frame?' Jas asks.

We 'sew' the material using a sharp rattan palm thorn to pierce holes in the cloth, then get Carly and Jody, who have the smallest fingers, to push and pull the thread through the holes and wrap it around the bamboo sticks, the way an old-fashioned boat has its mainsail attached to the boom. It's looking good, primitive but serviceable.

'Well done, girls, that's a marvellous job,' Jas says and they flush with pride.

'What shall we use for a tail?' Jody asks.

'I know, I know! Bonnie's journal. Tear out the pages and twist them into bows and tie them on string.'

'No way, May!'

But none of our other materials are light enough though. Paper it will have to be, but certainly not my journal. I pull Mum's book out of my rucksack.

I begin at the title page—*Zen and the Art of Motorcycle Maintenance, An Inquiry into Values*. I tear it out and twist it in the middle and tie it onto a long length of fishing line. Then I tear out the page that gives the name of the publisher. The page where Pirsig dedicates the book—FOR MY FAMILY. Next goes the Author's Note and the next page which has only these words '*And what is good, Phaedrus, And what is not good—Need we ask anyone to tell us these things?*' I tear out a dozen pages in all, worrying all the time about what Mum'll say when she sees her precious book ruined. As if it matters.

I loop another length of twine and attach it to both ends of the upright stick. This forms the bridle, the string to which the flying line is attached. We are lucky to have enough fishing line. I attach one end of the flying line to the bridle and the other end to a piece of driftwood.

'We must decorate it,' says Jody.

'It doesn't need decorating,' Jas replies.

'I know what it needs. May, where's your make-up?'

'What do you want that for, you stupid kid?'

'Give it here and I'll show you.' Jody snatches May's make-up bag and hands it to me.

'Lipstick's no good, it'll be invisible on the red. Anyway, I've lost my lipstick.'

Jody looks guilty.

I scratch the taut red fabric with a mascara-laden little brush, and write the letters SOS as large as possible.

'There,' I say. 'Phaedrus would be proud of me.'

'And who's Phaedrus when she's at home?' Arlene scratches the open sores on her arms.

'He . . . Just someone I know. A friend.'

I suppose carrying the kite to higher ground would be a good idea, but it's so windy on the beach I might as well try it here. The juniors are excited and want to help fly it. So I let Jody and Carly carry the kite along the sand as far as the string will stretch and then throw it into the air. It doesn't even take off, just flops onto the beach and lies like a dead exotic bird. They are too little to get any lift.

Jas tries this time and throws it into the wind. I turn on the fly line to try to give it height. For a few seconds it seems it will fly. It sways and lifts and tumbles, raises its crimson head and falls flat on its face. Jas follows it and sorts out the tangles before throwing it up again. It doesn't seem to have the correct lift somehow. I don't know why. Possibly the fabric is too heavy for the frame? Perhaps my design is faulty.

'One more time,' I shout to Jas.

She hurls the kite into the wind again and we watch it lift and turn, pulling against the line, the tail streaming in the strong wind.

'Hooray, it's flying!' Jody and Carly are jumping up and

down in glee. I'm hanging on like mad, running and letting out the flying line bit by bit, unfurling it from the stick. It's looking good, we have lift off. I lean against the wind and let the kite fly high. Something seems to be happening to it though. I can see red fabric being torn from the frame, like flickering flames, until the kite suddenly dips and falls to earth, sail-less, like a shot red bird. My sewing technique hasn't been good enough.

This failure is like all the others: those lost girls, the fires that failed, the sunk raft, Hope's death. Like the kite, we are plunged into utter despair.

'What now?' May asks me.

'Don't ask me, why is it always me that has to find solutions? You think of something for a change.'

'Sorry I spoke.' She walks away down the beach, picking up stones and hurling them into the water.

'Come on, let's go find some fruit.' Jas takes the broken kite from my hands and drags me to the tree line. Jody and Carly have retired to the banyan. I can't stop crying.

We take a different route into the forest in the hopes of finding fruit or nuts. There's a big clearing of crashed trees and a haze of new green growth blankets the muddy earth already. New life. Fig trees are everywhere. They aren't just trees, some are bushes and others are climbers. No wonder there are so many gibbons on this island. But most of the fruit is too high to reach and the trees too flimsy or branchless to climb.

'I think we are going to be stuck here for ever.'

'No, Bonz. That's mad. We only came for three nights. Our families will be desperate.'

'If they're still alive.'

'Don't say that!' she shouts at me. 'You mustn't give up hope. They'll come soon. They *are* looking, I'm sure. It's just that they don't realize that we drifted so far from the original island. We're closer to Cambodia than Thailand.'

'You think?'

'Yes, and I know we have to keep hoping and helping ourselves. Not give up.'

There's a sharp whooping and screeching, and a shaking of leaves above us, and a small infant gibbon falls crumpled at our feet. The mother peers down and *hoo-hoos* in alarm. The infant looks up at us in terror and then its eyes glaze over. It's dead.

'What a shame we haven't got a fire, we could cook it,' I say.

CHAPTER TWENTY-SEVEN

No sleep last night. I'm hungry.

The sea is red this morning. It moves sluggishly, falling in long folds like treacle. The sun has not yet risen and the sky is a ceiling of heavy violet clouds. Rain will come today again and we will have no fire to comfort us and be our beacon or wind to launch a kite. I sit thinking of my grandparents' house in Sutherland. I think of sweet chestnuts and potatoes roasting in the ashes of the fire. I can hear the blackened shells exploding; smell the comforting aroma of butter and black-peppered fluffy baked potato. My throat feels as if a stone is lodged there and I can't shift it.

A transparent crab appears from its small hole and starts shovelling sand. I wait. It moves away from the safety of its burrow and I grab it and put it straight into my mouth and crunch and swallow. I sit still, the wind stretching my hair behind me.

The sea is now purple.

I wait. Another crab comes within my reach and I eat it. I spit out the shell of this one, it's too crunchy to swallow. I eat six crabs in an hour. About the same amount of flesh as a small handful of peas but they'll have vitamins and minerals in.

The two juniors are hanging upside down from a banyan branch, getting in the way of Jas, who is trying to tidy our belongings in the enclosure. She is the only one who cares about our comfort, if you can call it that. She shakes the sand from our sleeping bags and sweeps the floor clean of leaves and bits of fruit skin.

We've seen evidence of rats lately in our camp. In the night they steal bits of coconut flesh and leave droppings under our sleeping bags. I expect they are nibbling away at Natalie's body and the boatman's remains too. We don't investigate; don't want to know.

Jody asks me to make a bow and arrow for her. 'We should have thought of it before—weapons, we need more weapons, in case . . . in case we need them,' I say to Jas. 'The juniors have lost their spears already.'

We gather several different sorts of thin bendy branches and Jas and I experiment. After a day of cut fingers and blistered thumbs I've made a bow. I don't know the name of the tree, but its damp twigs are springy and supple and bend beautifully. I secure string to the bow with a round turn and two half hitches at each end. Arrows are easier. I have whittled sticks to a sharp point, and at the other end I have cut a notch to fit into the line. I did try to make a feathered arrow from a piece of seabird feather, but it didn't work. I fasten guitar string around the ends of the bow. It makes a flexible bowstring, but when I try to fire the arrow it simply flops to the ground. There must be a better way. I draw pictures of arrows I've seen in movies. The correct flight has to be the answer. After walking up and down the beach several times looking for feathers I make several attempts to cut and fix them to the arrow. I think I've got it now. I split a feather from the top down the centre of the quill, leaving a little quill at each end to tie to the arrow. Tie three flights, equally spaced, around the shaft.

I draw a diagram of the bow and arrow in my journal.

'Here you are, Jody, catch us some supper.' I give her the weapon and watch her whoop and yell like a primitive native, leaping around the beach, Carly running after her.

Encouraged by my success, I put my mind to more ways of making weapons. A catapult should be easy. Having gathered several forked pliable twigs I choose the most sturdy specimen and cut it to size. Elastic is what is needed. We don't have any. Yes we do.

'Who's going to sacrifice their knickers for the sake of our survival?'

Jas looks alarmed.

'Don't worry, I'll do it.' I have shorts I can wear without my pants, so I remove the elastic and tie it onto the tops of the V. No, that won't do. It needs a pouch to fit pebbles in. I untie one end and slide a piece of doubled up T-shirt sleeve on. I gather some pebbles to use as missiles and practise my shooting skills.

Jas is looking even thinner—she says she's gone off coconuts. Hunger torments us. It doesn't matter how much fruit we eat, we are always hungry. We're not getting enough protein or carbohydrates or vitamins. No wonder we are listless and lacking in energy.

I find myself wandering into the forest. I'd love to tell Jas about the monk. I'm tempted to look for him despite my promise of silence. After all, he has pawpaw and breadfruit. He has chickens, a fire, delicious eggs. He would help us, I'm sure. Perhaps I could bring some of his fire back to the beach? Perhaps I should. Our survival is as important as his—more.

I keep to the paths we have made before, but not too deep into the forest. I see wild boar behind every tree, snakes hanging from every branch. There's no tiger to protect me. Figs here are small and puny. Jas explained once that they grow on climbers, beginning life as epiphytes, (plants that live off other plants) putting down roots, which eventually strangle the host tree. I've learnt so much since we were stranded here. I keep walking.

I go back to where I remember finding the bananas and cut a large bunch, which I throw over my shoulder and head back towards the beach again. I think it was around here that I saw the tiger and fell down into the monk's ravine, but I can't be sure. I whistle loudly, not because I'm happy but to warn wild boar and snakes that I am coming. I'm trying to be positive, but thoughts of Sandy's empty sleeping bag and the sight of the black fin in the lagoon, the crab crawling out of the boatman's eye socket, the billowing cloud of explosions, and Hope's flailing arm make a nightmarish patchwork in my head. In spite of the humidity and heat I am shivering.

I don't go looking for the monk.

I cannot put him in danger.

I promised.

'Look what I've got, look what I've got.' Jody is carrying a flapping blue fish on the end of an arrow. 'I caught it from the rocks. Aren't I clever? And Carly helped.'

'Good girls, well done!' Jas is always so upbeat, so

positive. I don't know where we would be if it wasn't for her. She's our surrogate mother. She shows Mrs Campbell up for the disaster that she is. I hate to think of her being hurt. I haven't said anything about her father and Loopy Layla, and I never will. What if it was my dad? Would I want to know?

I kill the fish, hitting its head on a rock. We watch the thin blood, pink, slipping into the water, then cut off the head, skin and fillet it, slice it thinly and squeeze lime juice over it and hang it in strips over a branch, watching red flies gather.

We've run out of salt.

But nothing is wasted. The juniors are using the empty cylindrical salt container as a pretend telescope.

211

Counted twenty-eight new mozzie bites. Got trench foot too, I suspect—something disgusting growing between my toes. This morning—heavy rain and strong wind. Sand everywhere.

Rain runs in rivulets down from the inadequate roof onto our sleeping bags. We get up; it's too uncomfortable to remain lying down. My teeth are mossy. Can't open my mouth without my lips cracking. My hair is like greasy string. The scratches and cuts are healing though; the monk's poultices worked well. My bruises have faded to a rather sickly yellow.

There is a huge swell, and the sea looks tall, as if there is too much of it for the space it has. The far out waves are dark green, fading to a paler jade in the shallows, the green-grey low sky is streaked with yellow and purple. It reminds me of pansies.

'Jas, Bonnie, come and look! Treasure!' Jody and Carly are very excited.

The tide line is covered in debris. Several ten-foot planks of wood, segments of corrugated roofing material of man-made fibre, crushed plastic water bottles with USAF markings, a bottle of unidentified sticky green liquid; a khaki canvas boot, size 12; an AA battery, corroded; a full crate of American beer; a thick red rubber glove and a single battered flip-flop. A large inner tube from a lorry or plane or something floats in and out on the waves. We gather it all together. Maybe there *has* been some sort of explosion on the base. It doesn't bear thinking about.

Jas and I keep everybody busy.

The roofing plastic goes on top of our multilayered roof. The crate becomes a seat and a table. The planks are very welcome as flooring over the mud. Carly has adopted the boot as her baby. She wraps it in her red neckerchief and hums nursery rhyme tunes to it. It's a shame we haven't fire. The rubber glove would make a good oven glove.

There is no point in going to find fruit in this weather. The forest is very dark; deep mud makes us slip and slide. We stay on the beach or go to the pool.

Jas is becoming an expert fisherman. She has more patience than anyone I know. She catches small fish from the rocks. Once they are seasoned with lime juice and hung to dry for a day or two, we guzzle on them, flies or no flies. Another source of protein is the sea cucumbers we find at low tide. They taste of nothing but seawater and the jelly texture is disgusting, but we have to eat something. Our limbs are shrinking; we look like the Holocaust survivors we've read about at school. Carly's and Jody's heads look too big for their skinny necks and bodies and because they've scratched their mozzie bites they've made them infected. I am even more of a stick insect than I used to be.

'Your ribs are like a half-built boat,' Jas teases me. Mum has always described Jas as voluptuous, but she would hardly recognize her now. She looks like another person, cheeks hollowed, hip bones sticking out. Sometimes she even looks like her poor mother.

I am wading in the shallows searching for more sea cucumbers when I look up and see Loopy Layla and the Barbie Babes staggering towards us. They all look rough.

'There've been wild boar at the cave. We're frightened. Is it all right if we move back with you into the encampment?' Mrs Campbell's eyes are wild, scared.

'I suppose so, it's not up to me.'

'We'll ask the others then.'

Jas and the juniors must have agreed because by the time I get back, Mrs Campbell and her acolytes have moved back in with us, much to my disgust.

'It's a good thing,' Jas tries to cheer me up. 'We ought to stick together, work together to survive.'

'But are they going to help? Or just be a liability again?' She shrugs.

I have forgotten about the crate of beer.

'What's this—beer? Where's the opener?'

'May Taylor, you aren't old enough to drink beer.'

'Poo to you, Bonnie Madam MacDonald, mind your own stupid business. Give me the opener.'

'Oh go on,' says Jas, 'let's have some. It'll make a change from water and coconut milk and it's not very strong. We could do with a light stimulant. It won't hurt, Bonnie.'

I am angry—feel let down by her, and isolated.

'Do what you like, I don't care.'

'What did the wild boar do, Mrs Campbell?' asks Jody.

'We woke to find two of them nosing around us. One had long tusks and small red eyes and they smelt real bad,' said Arlene.

'Not as bad as you do, Arlene. I expect they thought you were a new mate.' May hoots with laughter at her own joke and Arlene pushes her over. God I hate them. Wish the boar had eaten them all.

We drink the beer in one night. It's wonderful, fizzy and refreshing and makes me feel sleepy and carefree. They all laugh too much.

Morning, Day?

I have a sore head and feel sick and guilty. I think we sang songs but I don't really remember. I hope I didn't say anything about monks or tigers. It would be awful if he was arrested or removed from his island because of me. Oh, God, I hope I didn't give him away. The trouble is, I can't tell reality from fantasy any more. I drift into a sort of dream-state in order to escape from what's happening. I wonder if the others feel this way? Jas? I can't talk to Jas any more. I feel totally alone.

Life is uncomfortable inside the enclosure, and more cramped now the others are here. We are all bad-tempered with each other this morning. Especially me. I'm still very angry with our so-called leader. I blame her for everything that's gone wrong and I don't trust her. I don't know what triggered this memory—I had been trying to take my mind away from our predicament by thinking about happier times with Gran and Grandpa—but I had a sudden memory of Gran telling me that the Campbells and MacDonalds are born to be enemies. The feud between us dates back to 1500. The Campbells were rich and the MacDonalds notorious cow thieves. In 1692 the Clan Campbells massacred thirty-eight of the Clan MacDonald at Glencoe. We've been sworn enemies ever since. I remember Gran telling me stories about a man called Mad Colin Campbell—I expect Loopy Layla is descended from him. I felt better once I'd pulled all those bits and pieces of stories and history from my head. I knew that Gran would be pleased that I had remembered.

Layla disappears each day, to make and drink her coconut hooch, no doubt. May and Arlene do nothing but complain about everything—the heat, the cold, the rain, the wind, our diet of coconut, figs and raw fish, the mosquito bites, the sand flea bites, their dry lips and skin, their itching heads. Thank goodness none of us has had a period since Hope. We have no tampons or towels. It would be gross if we were bleeding all over the place. Jas reckons the trauma we've suffered and our limited diet stops our bodies functioning normally.

I am the one giving out orders, not Mrs Campbell. She tried but I wasn't having any.

'Bonnie, I think you and Jas should go back to the bananas and get us some. They're nutritious. You know where they are.'

'So? No way. I'm not going into the forest again. If you want some, you go. *You* get eaten by wild boar. *You* get bitten by snakes.'

She turns away from me, sighing loudly. I smell the stink of her unshaven armpits, the salt smell of her sticky hair, the stale drunk smell of her breath. She walks away along the beach in pants, petticoat and shredded blouse, her lean tanned body hunched and angry, arms folded over her breasts, and into the sea, wading out until the waves tumble over her as she hurls herself into the surf.

'Isn't that where the rip current is?' says Jas.

'So what? Stupid woman knows that, doesn't she?'

216

'Bonnie! What's happening to you? You used to be so caring. You sound so callous and angry.'

I walk away from Jas. My scowl is a permanent fixture these days.

Stubbing a toe, I swear and look back to see an arm disappear into the waves. Stupid cow, she's caught in the rip. She's trying to swim straight back in towards the shore but the rip is dragging her out. She deserves to die; it's not my problem. She killed Natalie. Dispassionately, I watch as she's swept out by the sullen sea.

'Bonnie, Bonnie!' Jas runs into the sea and starts swimming. She's not the world's best swimmer.

'No, Jas, come back.' I run straight into the water and throw myself after her. 'Go back. I'll get her.'

'Oh please, Bonnie, save her.' But Jas is caught in the rip too, and I shout to her to swim sideways in order to get out of it. I swim with her until she's obviously safe and heading in to shore.

Then I power out with my ace crawl and as I reach Layla Campbell I see she's in a bad state; she has swallowed water and is disorientated. I catch hold of her, but she struggles and I'm in danger of being pulled under by her. So I punch her hard in the face, enjoying her look of surprise as she slumps in my arms. I let the rip sweep us out, going with it, holding on to her all the time, limp now in my arms. She's heavier than she looks, she's bigger than me, and my arms are tired. I let my legs do the pumping, moving us gradually at right angles to the current. After about forty feet we are out of it, out of the frightening invisible rip. It's at this point that I have an overwhelming desire to let go of her, let her sink. I hate this woman. It would be so easy to allow her to drown. Everyone would think I had tried and failed to save her. I would be a hero for trying. She's limp in my arms, like someone dead. So I let go of her and she sinks like a rock. And I dive to reach her. Shit, she's heavy. I put my arm under her arm and chest and hold her head above water, swimming strongly on my back with her to shallow water where Jas waits to take her. Not until then do I remember the shark in the lagoon.

'I wish Layla Campbell had been eaten by the shark, and not Hope,' I tell Jas, panting. 'I wish it was Hope I had saved from drowning.'

Poor Hope. Did she realize? Was she aware of what was happening when the shark struck? Did she smell its fishy death-filled breath, feel its teeth tear at her flesh? Was she terrified? How long did it take for her to die? They say you don't feel a gross trauma injury at first. Pain comes later and she didn't have a later.

Mrs Campbell is face down on the sand, May and Arlene on their knees sobbing.

'Is she dead?'

'I hope so,' I say.

Jas is wrestling her into the recovery position and pumping her back. After a few moments water spews from her white lips and snot flows from her blue flared nostrils.

'Thank God,' says Jas.

Jody gently wraps a sandy sweatshirt around my shoulders and rubs them.

'You are very brave,' she says solemnly.

'Crazy, you mean.' I rub my hair and wipe my eyes. I'm crying again. Don't know why.

CHAPTER TWENTY-NINE

'Bonnie, I want to talk.' Mrs Campbell has appeared at my shoulder, as if from nowhere.

'What?' I bark.

'I want us to start again.'

'Why?'

'Bonnie, don't be like this.'

'Like what?'

'Angry all the time.'

'Say what you have to say.' I walk away from her along the beach and she has to run to keep up with me. Tiny transparent crabs flee from under my feet.

She grabs at my arm and I yank it away. 'Don't touch me.'

'Bonnie, you saved my life.'

'Yeah, well, you don't deserve to have your life saved.'

'Bonnie, I'm sorry, I'm sorry. Please stop and listen. I want you to understand.'

I look over my shoulder at her. She has tears on her cheeks; they could be real or maybe it's the wind. Her left eye is closed from the bruise where I punched her. She looks ugly. I'm glad.

'What do you want me to understand? That you're an alcoholic and a drug addict? You're selfish and a liar? You're a corrupter of minors? I know all that already.'

She slumps to the sand. I walk on.

She shouts after me, 'And you, Bonnie, what are you? You've condemned me without a hearing.'

I stop, sit down and look out at the dark grey sea, the white peaks and black troughs hiding the shark that killed Hope. I get up and walk back slowly to where she lies, a crumpled heap on the sand, her scarlet skirt like a dying rose, the petals brown-edged and ragged, spread out around her. Her face is in her hands, her chipped red nails pressed against her brow. She's sobbing.

I sit nearby, waiting and watching seabirds skim the waves, listening to their mournful cries. She eventually looks up and sees me, rubs her eyes and nose on her arm and sniffs loudly.

'I want you to understand, Bonnie. I want you to understand why I . . . why I'm . . . why I've been so . . . hopeless. My husband . . . my husband, Blaise . . . when he died,' she sobs and moans then contains her sorrow in a slow breath in and out, 'when Blaise died, I didn't want to live. I still don't want to live, at least I thought I didn't until you saved me.'

'That's no excuse for your behaviour here.'

'No, I know. I know, I'm sorry.'

I say nothing.

'I'm sorry too.' I don't sound sorry, I sound angry. I walk away from her, unable to comfort her, not knowing what I feel. She remains where I left her, collapsed on the sand, her head in her hands.

I find a rock and hide behind it to write up my journal. It's my only comfort, writing.

Why did I save her life? Because I knew Jas wouldn't manage to and she might have drowned? No, that's not all. I did it because it was the right thing to do. And I have been brought up to do the right thing. It would have been criminal not to save her life. I would have been just like her—not saving Natalie's life. Saving her was the Quality decision. Phaedrus knows what I mean, I hear his voice in my head: 'You have to do the right thing, no matter what.' I know forgiving her would also be the right thing to do. But can I do that? I can't even look at her.

CHAPTER THIRTY

After tasting the green liquid we found with the other flotsam delivered by the sea, we guess it's some kind of detergent. Mixed with water it foams. Terrific! We have soap and shampoo and take the opportunity to wash our hair in the stream, but we're careful not to use it all, we ration it, no longer taking anything for granted. This might be our only chance of being clean for a long time. The sudden cleanliness gives us a boost. We look more like our old selves. I even swill out my mouth with it. It's probably carpet cleaner or something, but who cares. It would be marvellous to have clean clothes, but we don't waste it on them, only our underwear. My period was surely due about now, but none of our bodies seem to be functioning normally. Just as well really.

Jody and Carly have found their own way out of chaos—they hold civilized tea parties with shells as cups and plates and blossoms as cakes. Jody is Daddy and Carly is Mummy. Two soggy teddies and Booty are being told to sit up straight and mind their manners. They walk them to school at the other end of the beach and give them lessons.

'Can I have some of your pages, please, Bonnie?'

'No.'

'Oh, please.'

'Pretend you've got paper.' Jody wanders off. Later I hear her again, shouting angrily at the teddies.

'Shall I get San—the other teddy bear to join you?' I ask, trying to be nice.

Carly looks horrified and shakes her head violently.

'We can't take Sandy's bear.' Jody looks at me as if I'm a criminal. 'It's waiting for her spirit in the cave. On our shrine.'

'OK. Sorry.'

Mrs Campbell is trying to make up for her previous lack of interest. She makes sure we all have plenty of fresh water, bullying the Barbie Babes to gather it from the stream that rises in the fringe of trees behind the beach. It's no big deal, no hardship, but she's doing it as a gesture that she cares. Jas is falling over herself to be pleasant to her. Toadying, some might call it.

Oh thank you, Mrs Campbell, that's so kind of you, Mrs Campbell, let me lick your arse, Mrs Campbell. Well, she might as well.

Mrs Campbell's even attempting to mother the juniors. Jody has a healthy suspicion of her but they've all been shell-hunting together, stringing orange coral beads onto strings of silky strands of black seaweed. But I notice that Carly isn't wearing her necklace. She has placed it on the shelf with the other spirit offerings.

Jody's a funny little thing. Every morning she stands to attention and sings the National Anthem solo—a real United States Air Force kid.

'*Oh, say, can you see, by the dawn's early light . . . ?*'

What we can see, and smell, by the day's morning light is

that the latrine is in a horrible state. We need to dig another, but we lost the shovel with the raft.

'Jas, perhaps your Mrs Campbell would like to take over latrine-digging duty?'

'*My* Mrs Campbell? Bonnie, don't be horrible. She's trying her best. We all make mistakes.'

'Some mistake! Allowing Natalie to die because she kept the whisky to herself!'

'Give her a chance, Bonnie.'

'Why?'

'Because I'm asking you.'

I can't quarrel with that.

CHAPTER THIRTY-ONE

May or early June '74 Koh Tabu
The stench from our original latrine is unbearable.

Miraculously the rain has stopped and the waves look less like mountain peaks than usual. The sun shines bravely through the dawn mist and the gibbons sing a cheerful operetta. A blue sky blesses us. After a communal breakfast of coconut milk and figs we creep away separately to crap wherever we can find in the forest and bathe in the stream. We've abandoned the overflowing latrine.

'I think it might be my birthday today,' said Jody.

'Your birthday? How old are you, dear?' Mrs Campbell asks. She's trying much too hard.

'Ten but I'm going to be eleven.'

'Eleven!'

'What date is your birthday?' I ask.

'The sixth of June.'

'Oh my God, have we been here that long?' I say.

'Happy Birthday, Jody!' Jas grabs and hugs her and Carly jumps up and down and starts singing very loudly, 'Happy Birthday to you, Happy Birthday to you . . . ' and we all join in, even me.

'Carly's talking again,' Jas whispers to me.

'We must celebrate,' says Mrs Campbell.

'How? With water and coconut?'

'No, with a dance, a party.'

'Yeah, yeah, a party!' The juniors bounce like Masai warriors.

So, we all go out looking for fresh fruit, fresh fish, fresh coconut. Jas uses seaweed to write in the sand:

JODY ELEVEN

'I wish Sandy and Natalie could be here for the party.' Carly begins to moan and cry softly, hugging herself and rocking as she sits on the sand. Jas hugs her. 'Hope, too.'

'Jody's here, Carly. Mikey's here,' she says.

'No he isn't, don't be silly. Mikey's dead.'

'Is he, Jody? How did he die?' I ask her.

'A wild boar ate him.'

There is an uncomfortable silence. I go cold. The juniors are better at expressing their fears than the rest of us, it seems.

'Aren't you going to look at your presents?' says Mrs Campbell.

'Presents?' Jody's eyes light up. We have all found treasures to give her. I have found the skeleton of a tiny bird, bleached white, wing bones still attached. Jas has found a pile of tiny pink tellin shells and tells Jody they are mermaids' fingernails. Carly gives her a white feather. May says she will do her hair for her until they are rescued; Arlene has plaited a bracelet from coconut husk and threaded it with little blue shells. Mrs Campbell has strung the inner tube up to a leaning palm to make a swing.

We all sit around on the beach and drink coconut milk and eat figs and a really special treat—eggs. I found eggs in the nest above where the baby bird skeleton lay. Don't know what bird the nest belonged to, but whatever it was laid six tiny blue-green eggs. I took five and left one. It's a terrible shame we have no fire. We have to eat them raw. But to make them more palatable we mix them into the coconut milk and pretend it's milkshake. Jas has made a sand cake decorated with shells. Eleven twigs represent candles. We gather round it and tell Jody to blow out the candles. She puffs out her cheeks and blows hard and we sing 'Happy Birthday' again and all clap Jody, who does look pleased. Little rituals like this are important for our wellbeing. A comfort, where comforts are few.

'I must keep an eye out for birds' nests,' I tell Jas. 'Eggs are a good source of protein. Toucan's eggs must be really big.'

She smiles at me. We haven't spoken much of late.

'Jas, where do toucans nest, do you know?'

She bursts out laughing. 'You really want to know?'

I nod. I can tell she's enjoying this.

'Well, after mating the male walls up his mate alive inside a tree-hole and feeds her through a small hole, which is just big enough to take his bill. When the young fledge the mother breaks out and they follow.'

'It would be like breaking and entering!'

So, no toucan eggs for us then.

Mrs Campbell pretends to play the ruined guitar, drumming with her knuckles on the surface, and plucking the remaining string.

'Name a tune!' she calls us round.

Jody chooses 'Teddy Bears' Picnic'. We all choose 'Imagine', 'Let it Be' and 'Bridge over Troubled Water'. We dance together in pairs like old ladies at old-fashioned dances. I partner Jody and Jas dances with Carly standing on her feet. I remember suddenly that I did that with Daddy when I was little. I wonder if I'll ever see him again.

Mrs Campbell finishes with a solo—'My Sweet Lord'. We're all crying by the time she finishes 'Hare Krishna, Hare, Hare'. The sand is mussed up by our dancing feet.

It's been a successful party, even without real cake, candles or fire.

Jas isn't content to leave the bird skeleton simply as something beautiful to look at; to Jas it's a teaching tool. We all sit around under the banyan's spreading branches, where we spend most of our time these days, and she points out to us the various bones and what they are called and their purpose.

'You see this bone here? The radius it's called. That's the ulna, and that's the humerus. We have the same bones on our arms and elbows.'

'Humerus? Is that where the funny bone is?'

'I suppose that could be where the expression originated.' We laugh.

'You make a good teacher, Jas.'

'Thanks, Mrs Campbell. What did you do before you were married?'

'Me? Not a lot. After I left drama school in London I went to Los Angeles—tried to be an actress but spent most of my time working as a waitress in a diner.'

'Were you in Hollywood?' asks May.

'No, I never got any parts in movies.'

A failed actress—that figures. 'What made you interested in survival skills?'

'What makes you think I am?'

'Someone said you were.'

'Well, people say a lot of things about me that aren't true.' She laughs and pushes her sticky hair from her face. 'Anyway, isn't it time you called me Layla? Mrs Campbell makes me feel so old.' I look at her. She has bags under her swollen eyes, her arms are thin, her lips are cracked, her clothes ragged, but her beauty surfaces with her smile. It's the sort of smile that makes us all smile.

'Is that where you met your American husband, Layla? Los Angeles?'

'Yes, he's . . . he was from LA. Used to come to the diner and couldn't resist my Scottish accent.' She smiles, sadly. I'd like to ask her more questions but before I can, she continues, 'While we're all together, I really think we should be making a plan.'

'What sort of plan?' asks May, who is weaving Jody's straggly hair into dozens of tiny plaits.

'We have a choice. We either make life as comfortable as we can on the island, assuming we are going to be here for a very long time . . . '

'But we are going to be found,' I interrupt. 'You all seem to have become resigned to being here for ever.'

'Or,' she says, ignoring me, 'we make a plan to get off.'

'We've tried a raft, and you know what happened.' I am suddenly angry with her again. She has reminded me of my part in Hope's death. Not that I need reminding. I'll never forget the arm raised for help and the scream like a lost seabird.

'Yes, and it was very brave of you and Hope. Very courageous. But we have to try again. Or attempt to light a fire without matches. Yes, yes, I know, it's my fault we have no matches. But the weather hasn't helped.'

'What do you suggest?' asks Jas.

'Well, what about one of us using the inner tube as a flotation aid and swimming off for help?'

By 'one of us' she has to mean me, as I'm by far the best swimmer. The shark speeds through my head and strikes me. I shudder. Why should I have to be the one who risks my life again?

'That's a stupid crazy idea. You've forgotten the shark.'

'I think we should try to light another fire,' says Jas.

'How do you intend to do that?' I say, listening to the rain on the corrugated roofing—it sounds heavier than it did on the thatch or bamboo roof and runs in waterfalls onto our floor as we huddle together in the middle.

'I've been thinking about that. I remember a boy's book I had once. I think it said you could scratch a knife blade on rough rock to make a spark,' Jas replies coolly

'Sounds worth a try. OK, girls, let's go find the perfect rough rock.' Mrs Campbell jumps to her feet and leads the way out into the rain. We follow like good little girls. After about half an hour we have a little pile of likely looking rocks in the camp. I choose a blade from the Swiss army knife and practise scratching it on the roughest stone. Nothing happens.

'It doesn't work. I'm just blunting the knife.'

'Let's try the other knife—the boatman's knife. It's got a bigger blade.' Mrs Campbell hands it to me.

Nothing happens for a while, then there's a smell of scorching. All eyes are on my hands, scraping back and forth. I keep on and on and in the darkness of the enclosure I see a tiny spark.

'Jas, it works. You're brilliant! Get lots of wood and twigs, the drier the better. Let's get to work.' I'm so excited that my voice squeaks. I am desperate to build a fire straight away.

But Mrs Campbell holds up the palms of her hands and my mood plummets.

'I suggest we build a fire on higher ground and keep it going,' she says, oozing calm. As far as I'm concerned she might as well have said, 'You're just kids and know nothing.' I want to scream at her but one look from Jas and I rein myself in.

'That was what we were trying to do ages ago, for goodness' sake.'

'Yes, but this time we know a bit more about the island and can choose the best place for the fire and we can *all* tend it.'

'That's what you said last time.' I can't believe her cheek. Doesn't she realize that I nearly died trying to build that fire? My Quality fire.

'Bonnie, shh!' Jas slaps my arm.

'What about fierce animals?' says Jody.

'We'll take weapons and make a lot of noise,' says Mrs Campbell.

'I've got a bow and arrow.'

We have spears, a bow and arrow, catapult, and a sling-shot that Jas has made of string and a flip-flop toe piece. The boatman's curved steel blade can be strapped back on to the cork handle, once we've finished using it as our sparking steel.

'Bonnie, where do you think is the best place for a signal fire, remembering that we have to make camp close by so we can keep it going?'

Ha! Now she thinks my opinion is worth having. I want to yell abuse at her, but something tells me that now is not the time. There are other people to think about. I take a deep breath.

There follows what can only be called a civilized discussion in which we weigh up our options. Jas keeps smiling at me, encouraging the Nice Bonnie to stay in touch, to contribute.

So, after a while, it's decided. Layla, Jas, and I will trek to Fire Mountain, light a signal fire and keep it going night and day as long as the weather holds. The juniors will stay on the beach with May and Arlene.

'Who's looking after the juniors, then?' I mutter to Jas, and she just smiles, thankful here hasn't been another row.

'You wouldn't want that air moaning their way through the island,' she says. 'This is definitely the best solution.'

We watch Carly and Jody run off to make an SOS on the sand and the rest of us start organizing things for the big trek.

I decide to practise with the sparking while we're still on the beach as there really should be a fire here too. Then any fish or shrimps can be cooked and they'll have more security from wild animals. I scrape and scratch the steel blade onto the rough side of a large rock in the shelter of our encampment.

'We'll have to find a smaller stone,' I say to May, who is watching.

'OK.' She wanders off and comes back with just the right size and type of rock.

I'm surprised and she hears it in my voice when I thank her.

'We're not as useless as you think, Bonnie MacDonald,' she hisses.

Having gathered a small amount of tinder—lichen mostly, and moss, I set light to it from the sparks. Oh, the magic of fire! I set twigs on top, calling to the juniors to help and soon we have a decent campfire. The recent dry spell means some of the timber is dry. We throw coconut husks on; they burn well.

The fire brightens our faces and lifts our mood.

'Don't just stand looking,' Jas shouts, 'let's catch some supper!'

We have a frenzy of fishing with the net on a stick, the spear and the arrow. Before long we have several small fish and shrimp—a feast. I spear the fish on sharpened sticks and roast them on the fire. We boil the shrimp in a shell of water.

The juniors have stuck feathers in their hair and painted their faces with lipstick and ash. They look tanned and skinny and fierce. After the feast they chase Jas and me around the beach, whooping and yelling and brandishing weapons. It's good to see them cheerful. I think about Hope and how she gave them towel rides on the sand. I think about what has changed—no Sandy, no Natalie, and no Hope.

233

But I'm glad we have a plan.

Mrs Campbell writes out a list of campfire watchers, and the rest of us go to bed with optimistic thoughts for once.

CHAPTER THIRTY-TWO

Hope is calling out, screaming, her face half eaten, one arm and leg gone, the water dark with blood. She swims towards me, brain matter spilling out of her half-eaten head. I turn away. I'm sinking.

My own strangled groan wakes me. Sweat runs down my forehead into my eyes. I struggle out of the sleeping bag. I can't smell the fire, but it's all right. Mrs Campbell is sitting close to it, her eyes fixed on the glowing ashes. I go into the forest and wash using a tiny dribble of detergent. It's wonderful the difference soap makes. I feel almost human again. I clean my teeth with a twig, and swill out my mouth with water. Clambering over a fallen tree I rip off a dead branch and carry it back to the fire.

'Did you sleep?' Mrs Campbell asks.

'Yes thanks, fairly well.' I sit with her in silence. I wonder how it will feel to be adult. Is everything as easy as I think it is, black and white, right or wrong? How would I feel if I had lost a husband? I can't imagine it. I can't imagine what it would be like if my parents were dead. I would be lost. I suppose that alcohol and drugs might seem like the best escape from that sort of pain.

'You don't really think there's been an air strike on the base, do you?'

'I hope not, Bonnie. But, you know, there are rumours, well, more than rumours. The North Vietnamese army is pushing south at a great rate. Cambodia is involved too.' She points at the nearest coast. 'The South Vietnamese can't hold out for ever, and America is no longer prepared to support them, they're moving troops out. It's going to end badly.'

'You mean they've lost the war against the communists?'

'America is getting out.'

'Abandoning them?'

She shrugs. I try to digest what she's saying. We sit silently, watching the glow of the embers.

'I don't believe they'd just abandon them,' I say, eventually. 'My dad says that they're fighting for freedom, fighting against the communists, and their repression.'

'I'm sure . . . I'm sure that's what he believes,' she says quietly.

I don't want to take offence, but I don't understand what she means.

'Beware of loving a warrior, Bonnie.'

'A warrior? What do you mean?' It sounds like a quote from a history book or from Shakespeare or someone. 'Like a soldier?'

'Yes. They become brutalized by the casual violence of war.'

Was that another quote? 'My dad's an instructor . . . ' I say, and she nods.

There is a long silence.

'Is that what happened with your husband?'

She nods slowly, her face hidden from me.

'But I thought you loved him?'

'I did . . . at first.'

'Did you love Jas's father?' I can't help myself.

She stares at me, shocked. 'How did you—?' Then sobs, her face in her hands, shakes her head and doesn't answer.

'It's over, anyway,' she says eventually. 'I was mad. Stupid. It should never have happened. If we get out of here I'm going home to Aberdeen.' She takes a deep breath and says, 'God, I need a cigarette. Does Jas know about . . . ?'

I shake my head.

We sit for a while in silence.

'Mrs Campbell, Layla . . . '

'Yes, Bonnie?'

'The raft . . . Hope built it . . . She wanted me to wait until the wind dropped but I wouldn't. I didn't want to wait. I wanted to be heroic, save everyone. I made her come with me, and I couldn't steer through the reef and we were wrecked. She had no chance, you see, once she was in the water, she couldn't see . . . couldn't see where she was swimming. Her eyes . . . She had no chance. And it's all my fault, my fault.' Emotion overwhelms me.

She gathers me in her arms and I smell her hair and sour sweat. Tears and snot flood my throat. I'm choking. I want my mother and father. In my mind I see little Sandy with her teddy and Natalie with her comfort blanket, and poor brave Hope who had overcome her stutter and built a raft. I sob for all of our dead and for myself, for my guilt and my arrogance, for Jas and her mother, for what feels like the end of my childhood.

When my sobbing subsides, I pull away from her. She looks exhausted and old and sad.

'You must be tired. Better get some rest. We'll be setting off today won't we?'

'Thanks, Bonnie, I will.' She touches me on the shoulder as she rises.

The fire has a solid base and I check that there's enough wood and coconut husks to last as fuel for several days. I gather figs and fresh water for breakfast and the others wake and join me. Layla sleeps on.

'Let her sleep,' I say. 'She'll need all her energy for the climb.'

Jas raises an eyebrow at me.

We are travelling light. Just the weapons, the knives, water, of course, and sleeping bags. I carry my rucksack, with my journal, pencil, and what's left of my Robert M. Pirsig. Can't travel without them. We'll gather food when we need to. No point in loading ourselves unnecessarily. We have the broken mirror wrapped in a banana leaf and the sparking stone and some twine.

Arlene and May, Carly and Jody wave us goodbye. The junior war-paint is smudged over their faces. I think Jody is near to crying. She hugs Jas and then me.

'This time stay here,' I say sternly.

'It was Mikey's fault, not mine, he made me go.'

'You shouldn't speak ill of the dead,' I say.

'Bonnie! That's in very bad taste,' says Jas, smiling at me, then to Jody, 'OK, OK, just be good and help with the fire and do what you are told, all right?'

'Yes, Jas.'

'You must be sure to keep the fire going, girls, don't let the juniors go into the sea, and pray it doesn't rain.'

'Yes, Layla.'

'And if anything bad happens to Jody or Carly while we're away I'll kill you.'

'Oh piss off, Bonnie MacDonald.'

'They'll be OK, don't worry,' says Arlene. 'We'll look after them.'

We have two flashlights, the beach group also have two. They have their own spears and bow and arrow, but we have both knives and the other weapons.

'See you later, alligator,' I call as they wave us goodbye.

'In a while, crocodile.'

Hours later, we are making good time, as we more or less know the direction we have to take. Most of the ribbons are still where I tied them and the forest hasn't had time to grow back over the paths we took, although across some paths tendrils and shoots are surreptitiously claiming back the jungle.

Tiger Cave is as I remember. No tiger this time, though, and no hornets, thank goodness. I tell Layla I've named it the Cave of Hands. It's difficult not to mention the tiger especially as there is a tiger drawing on the cave wall. The others are very impressed by the paintings, especially the giant hand.

'Why didn't we see the pictures that first time?' Jas wonders, and I mutter about the hornets and wanting to press on.

'There's a cave in the north of Thailand that has

paintings—Spirit Cave. It was only discovered recently—in the sixties; someone called Chester Gorman, an archaeologist.'

'How do you know all these things, Jas?'

'She's a genius, didn't you know?' I say proudly, doing a high five with Jas.

'If only we had a camera!' says Layla.

'I've drawn them in my journal.' I show the others my crude representation of the tiger, the hunters, the hands. Jas puts a hand on top of one of the smaller hand paintings on the wall.

'They were very small people,' she says. It's true; her hand is bigger than the cave hands.

'Who did that one?' asks Layla, pointing to the large hand—none of us can reach it.

'I bet no one else knows about this place,' Jas says.

'Who made the large handprint though?' says Layla.

I say nothing. We stay in Tiger Cave for the night. It's starting to rain again and it's the only shelter I know of in the area.

The old birds' nests on the cave floor make excellent tinder. I get a spark quite quickly this time and light a small fire in the entrance. As the fruit bats settle in the trees around us and white egrets sweep in to roost, we settle down in our sleeping bags and listen to the sounds of nightfall; the loud rattling hiss of cicadas, the monkeys screeching and the gibbons' communal sing-songs, the unidentified snorts and yelps and whoops. Jas points out the sound of the frogs chirping. Jas and I are old jungle hands, now. We talk a lot and laugh loudly at our own jokes. It helps keep the ghosts away.

Shadows dance high on the cave wall; the small hands

240

flicker as if they are waving to me, and the big hand flashes. I'm glad I'm not alone.

Hope is swimming towards me but she has no legs and no eyes. She screams, 'Help me! Bonnie, help me!'

I wake in a sweat and find Jas feeding the fire. The deep shadows under her eyes are exaggerated by the glow and her mouth looks sad. 'Shall I take over? It's nearly time for my watch.'

'No, it's all right. I'm not the least bit sleepy. Hungry though.'

'It's not breakfast time yet. You'll have to wait.' I wag my finger at her.

'What I wouldn't give for a hot chocolate.'

'Mmm, with a jammy doughnut.'

'A doughnut!'

'Mmm, and a thick slice of toast with honey and peanut butter.'

'Oh stop!' My mouth is watering.

'Coconut?'

'No, please, not coconut!' We giggle.

'God, I'd kill my grandmother for a whole roast chicken with roast potatoes, sausage stuffing, peas and gravy,' I tell Jas. 'D'you know what Gran says when she's hungry? She says, "I could eat a scabby wee bairn."'

Jas laughs at my hammed up Scottish accent, and Layla stirs in her sleep.

'No shortage of scabby bairns here,' Jas says.

* * *

241

As we start the day's climb, my thoughts turn to Layla. She's been quiet, treating Jas and me like an equal, almost.

I suppose it was a sort of hero worship I had, we *all* had, for Layla Campbell. She's pretty and tragic, like a heroine in a romantic novel. The kind of novel Mum despises. I realize I'm thinking about her as if she were dead. But perhaps my idea of who she was is dead. She's kooky, a hippie, unusual, not like my mum or the other USAF wives. She has—*had*—a glamour about her, a mystery. But she let us down.

Mum says everyone needs heroes. She says it's good to have someone to look up to and admire. Like the boxer Cassius Clay—or Muhammad Ali as he wants to be called now. Dad used to really like him until he refused to join the US Army, a conscientious objector. Now he despises him. 'Draft dodger,' he calls him. But Ali refused to join the army because war is against the teachings of the Holy Quran. So I admire him for it. It's not draft dodging. It's against his Islam principles to fight in a Christian war. He said, 'I haven't got anything against those Vietcong. No Vietcong ever called me "Nigger".'

It's just one more thing that Dad and I disagree about. I have a poster of Muhammad Ali on my bedroom wall. I've also got one of Mahatma Gandhi. Daddy never comes into my room, but if he ever did, and he saw them, he'd go mad. I don't care. Mum agrees with me that it's none of their business how I decorate my room. As long as I don't paint it black.

I'd do anything to be back home with them. I'd even paint my room pink if that's what he wanted.

242

CHAPTER THIRTY-THREE

Fire Peak, Koh Tabu, June '74
It turns out that Fire Peak is not far from the Cave of Hands and
we get here without mishap. I must have gone the long way
round the first time. The other two are a bit slower than me at
climbing but I showed them the best way up and we all carried
tinder and firewood. It's so much easier with three of us.

The fire was lit after only a few tries. Our spark stone works
brilliantly. I wonder what the monk uses for fire? He probably
only has the under-earth oven as he doesn't want to advertise
his presence with smoke. What a lonely strange life he must
have, but beautiful too. I think of the tiger lying next to him. It
was like that painting of a saint, maybe Saint Anthony, or
Daniel, I can't remember, surrounded by tigers and lions and
their prey lying in peace and harmony with each other. An idyll.
A part of me wants to talk about the monk but I must be discreet.
If the world gets to know about him and his tiger he'll be in
mortal danger. I mustn't ever mention him. He must be
protected from the outside world. No one must ever read this
journal.

We stay by the fire for two days and two nights and only see one
ship, a long way away. Two small craft, local fishing boats, have
been closer, but have gone on by. No planes.

Jas worries about Jody and Carly, and like me, doesn't trust May and Arlene to cope if anything goes wrong—like an attack by wild boar.

Layla's pulling her weight. We have found bananas and coconut, and although we are bored to death with them, they keep us alive. We'll have to go back down soon anyway as we are running out of water. My clothes are disgustingly smelly again but the wind at night is cooler up here and we need to wear everything we've got. Mostly we huddle in our sleeping bags on the flat rock close by the fire.

'I'm going to look for fresh water,' I say, taking one of the empty containers. It would mean that we could keep the fire going for longer. I hack my way through uncleared forest and nearly tread on a fallen nest with a clutch of quite big eggs. A feast of scrambled eggs. Or could be if we had a frying pan. I try to pick them up but one of the eggs is broken and I get the mess all over my hands. It's so sticky I can't wipe it off. Sticky! That's it! Glue. We have glue! We can make a successful kite now; glue it together. Phaedrus would be proud of me, working it out, thinking things through. Carrying the eggs in my T-shirt I get back to the others and tell them my plan. It's a good one, they agree.

'Shall we make it here or wait until we get to the beach?'

'It has more chance of being seen if we fly it here. It will go higher than it could go from the beach. More chance of being seen.'

'OK, but let's eat some now.' Jas looks desperate.

'Not raw, please, I can't stand it.'

244

'Watch this.' Layla uses the handle of the knife to chip away gently at the rounded top of an egg until she has broken away a dime sized piece of shell. 'Now the egg can cook in its own little pan without exploding.' She places the egg, pointed side down, in the embers of the fire, and repeats the process with two more eggs. We sit over the fire watching them cook. After about twenty minutes we use twigs like chopsticks to pick up the eggs and remove them from the fire. When the shells have cooled a little we peel the eggs and eat them. It's the most delicious food I have ever eaten.

'Where did you learn that?' I ask. Perhaps she's a survivor after all.

She shrugs. 'My aunt Aggie, maybe. She was a Girl Guide.'

We search for the right sort of springy thin bamboo for the kite, split it and make twine from split palm leaves. We already have some twine with us from beach finds. What to use as the fabric? Nothing we have is light enough. I'm pretty sure that that was my mistake before. Paper would be better. I find a relatively sheltered spot at the foot of the rocks and begin to tear out more pages of *Zen and the Art of Motorcycle Maintenance*. I dip each page into a coconut shell of raw egg and paste them together, sticking them onto the diamond shape framework, reading the pages as I go. I get to the part where Phaedrus's son has died.

Page 422. *Now Chris's body, which was part of that larger pattern, was gone. But the larger pattern remained . . . If you take that part of the pattern that is not the flesh and bones of Chris and call it the 'spirit' of Chris or the 'Ghost'*

245

of Chris, then you can say without further translation that
the spirit or ghost of Chris is looking for a new body to
enter.

Phaedrus and his wife have another baby, called Nell, and Chris's spirit lives on in her. I wonder if Hope's spirit will live on, if her parents have another child, or Sandy's wandering spirit will be at rest in another body. Buddhists believe in perpetual reincarnation, Lan Kua told me. I'm not sure what I believe.

I fit the strings onto the back, knotting bits of string and hand-made bark twine together. Then I make the tail using the rest of the pages. Phaedrus would be proud if he could see me now.

Carrying my precious cargo on my back I climb back to the top of the rock. The fire is only just burning and not a great deal of smoke rises high. It mostly gets blown away across the island like thin grey mist. Two small fishing boats head past the island way out beyond the reef. Layla and Jas have been jumping up and down, waving their arms, but we all know it's hopeless and that they won't be seen.

Layla takes the kite and walks as far away as she can on the flat rock. I hold the flight string tightly coiled around a stick. As she hurls it into the air I pull and lift, pull and lift until our bird flies high. It wavers once but rises at last until the string is at its last foot or so. We stand gazing up at it, our signal kite. Our freed bird. No SOS on it this time, no lipstick or mascara, just the many wise words of Robert M. Pirsig. Will anyone see?

'Who wants the rest of the water?' Layla offers an almost empty canister.

'You have it,' I tell Jas.

'Ugh! It's gasoline!' Jas spits. 'We must have brought the wrong bottle!'

'Give it here.' As quick as a flash I exchange the kite for the can. 'Get away both of you, run!'

'What are you doing?'

'Just get out of here!'

I hurl the gasoline onto the smouldering bonfire and throw myself as far away from it as I can, crawling along on all fours on the rock, following Jas and Layla. Blue flames leap into the sky.

I do believe the boats are coming closer. Yes, yes. Have they seen the flames or the kite? Will native boats land on an island that is taboo? We lose sight of them behind trees. They are still many hours away.

'Come on, let's go back. It'll take us at least a day, don't forget.'

'No, we can go faster downhill. I know the way. Come on!' Abandoning our fire but taking the kite, sleeping bags and rucksack we hurry back down. Layla gets winded very quickly.

'It's all that smoking,' I can't help saying.

'Yeah yeah, I know,' she puffs. 'It's my new year's resolution—to give up.'

'But it's June already,' says Jas.

'Don't waste breath, hurry!'

At one point we come to a thirty-foot drop where there's a waterfall. I have lost us. If we have to climb around it it will take hours as the forest is so thick, and we'll have to hack our way through.

'The waterfall,' I say. 'The only way to do this is to go straight down it.'

'How?'

I rip a vine from a tree near the top and hang on to it as I walk down backwards through the water. The others follow. We've saved a lot of time coming this way and if we follow the stream we will get to the beach in an hour or so.

Gibbons *hoo-hoo* at us from branches and toucans peer over their large bulbous beaks. At one point deer run from our path. Dhole bark. We pass the temple and the Cave of Hands, the mineral lick, the ferny clearing. Cicadas sing shrilly. All is a dream on this descent, a speeded up movie of jungle life; we fall over trailing branches and the massive roots of fig trees; scratched, cut, bruised. My beautiful kite is ripped on thorns, but I carry its remains, as if it's an injured bird. Layla is crying with exhaustion and has to stop to catch her breath. Jas waits for her while I continue alone, running now. A quick drink at the stream and on I go.

At last, covered in sweat, blood, and mud, thorns in my legs and arms, and covered in bites, I come to the beach.

CHAPTER THIRTY-FOUR

Jody runs to me along the beach, followed closely by the others. 'A boat, a boat! Bonnie, a boat!'

I'm sobbing. I haven't the breath to speak.

'It's coming to take us home.' Carly is unrecognizable. They all are. Carly has clean hair, clean face, and clean clothes, even clean fingernails. Bitten to the quick—but clean. Her face is covered in carefully applied make-up, as is Jody's. Arlene and May have obviously had a ball giving them 'makeovers'. They have looked after them after all.

Miraculously, the campfire is still alight.

The first boat is negotiating the reef. It sweeps through and putters in on its outboard motor. The other boat appears, rising on a wave and sliding through the reef, perched on the rolling waves. Jas and Layla come out of the trees. We all run together towards the first boat as it reaches the shore.

'Bonnie, Bonnie!'

'Mum, Dad!'

I can't believe it. My parents climb and stumble over the side of the boat, followed by Jas's mum and dad. I fall into my mother's arms.

'We've found you, we've found you.'

I'm not dreaming. The other boat beaches and Jody's and

Carly's parents, and Hope's mother, jump over the sides onto the sand. Jas's parents are holding Jas and crying. A short man with a crew-cut and a woman with tight black curls stagger ashore. Arlene and May run to them.

'Mum, Pa!'

'Hope, where's Hope?' Hope's mother shrieks. I cannot look at her.

'Layla?' Jas's father grabs Layla by the shoulders.

Jas's mother stares in surprise and incomprehension.

Layla falls to her knees, holding herself, sobbing.

Carly starts crying, 'Sandy, Sandy!'

Then Jody lets out a loud wail—'Natalie!'

I say, 'I'm sorry. I'm sorry. Hope . . . Hope's gone too.' And we are all of us weeping and weeping.

CHAPTER THIRTY-fivE

August 1974 Thailand
Following a brief hearing at a Coroner's Court in Bangkok the
three deaths were deemed to have been by misadventure. There
was a funeral for Natalie at the Catholic Church at Utapao, and
funerals without bodies for Sandy and Hope. In Sandy's coffin
was her teddy and her neckerchief, and in Hope's coffin her
silver crucifix and chain. We all attended the funeral of the
boatman. His family wanted to know everything he had said
to us. Everything he had done on the fateful voyage. Layla
told them he had courageously navigated the boat to an island
with fresh water and had helped us with our camp even though
the island was taboo. He had probably lost his life trying to
save us. That is what she said. We placed jasmine garlands in
the spirit house of his family and gave rice to the local temple
monks.

My dad paid to have the outboard motor repaired and gave it
to the boatman's family.

'We'd been searching since the storm, Puss,' Dad told me,
stroking my face as our sad party made its way home.
They wouldn't accept that I had perished, Mum said. No
one realized that there was a problem for a couple of days

251

because there had been a terrible incident at the base. One of our F52 bombers had crash-landed during the hurricane and the only runway was out of action. The bomber had crashed into other planes.

'There was extensive loss of personnel as well as machines.'

(He meant that lots of people had died. I'd almost forgotten that Dad spoke like that.)

'Then we went in search of the boatman, of course,' Mum explained. 'But the conditions were dreadful, and his village had been flattened in the tropical storm. Eventually, with the help of a translator we got hold of his son and one of his brothers—they were about to make a search for him. They weren't even aware that he'd taken you to the island.'

Mum kept swallowing hard. There had been three helicopters and a small reconnaissance plane from the base sent out immediately they realized that something was wrong to search for us, but because there had been some heavy fighting they couldn't be spared more than once.

'It was like a nightmare,' Mum said. Again and again, Dad had asked permission to take leave so that he could co-ordinate the search but all leave had been cancelled.

The boatman's family first had to make repairs to their boats, which had suffered severe damage in the storm. They guessed that his engine had probably broken down— it wasn't the first time apparently—and that he may have drifted. Eventually they began their search.

'On one occasion we think they had seen the flash of a mirror . . . '

'That would be May's,' I explained.

'But they didn't think too much of it, it was so brief,'

Mum said, 'and they didn't believe you could be so far from where you were supposed to be.'

Then our fathers were finally given leave of absence and they demanded that the boatmen take them further out, to the more distant islands. As far as Koh Tabu. They were just giving up hope when Jas's dad saw through his binoculars the kite soaring high on the same mountain where the boatmen had earlier seen the flash. There was also a whisper of smoke and then the sudden leaping blue flames. As they got closer to the reef they saw a huge SOS written on the sand and girls waving.

CHAPTER THIRTY-SIX

The South Vietnamese surrendered on 30 April 1975. There was a major evacuation of US personnel from Saigon using helicopters with F2 fighters as back-up. Dad was involved in that, though he never talks of it. But then, he never talks about his war anyway.

Cambodia was taken over by Pol Pot and the Khmer Rouge and it was reckoned that over 50,000 Buddhist monks were killed.

By then Mum and I were back home in Scotland. As my grandmother kept reminding me, I was much too thin. I was experiencing flashbacks to Hope's death and still having nightmares all the time. I was scared to go to sleep because of the dreams, from which I woke screaming. Mum encouraged me to read a lot of poetry. I discovered the poems of Ted Hughes and Elizabeth Bishop, and I began attempting to write poetry through the long nights. It was nothing like the love poems I once wrote to Lan Kua.

A holiday somewhere quiet was prescribed by my doctor.

October 1975, Sutherland, Scotland
Staying with my grandparents. They're stuffing me with porridge

every morning. I'm writing bad poetry. Walking lots. Today Grandpa's taking me fishing.

The air is clean and cold and smells of heather and freshly cut peat, and the sky is a pale robin's egg blue scratched with cirrus clouds the colour of orange peel. A weak sun shines. The only sound is of loch water lapping against the sides of the boat, and the mew of a red kite high above. Clouds of midges skim the peaty water and a fish rises, kisses the surface and leaves circles within circles. The low sun hits the raised edges of the ripples and turns them the colour of blood.

My grandpa sculls the little boat along smoothly. His eyes read the peaty water all the time, searching for the best place to fish, looking for signs on the surface to tell him what goes on beneath. He stops and we drift with the breeze. The far blue hills have a mist around them, like fire-smoke. We are the only people on the water and there are no fishermen on the banks. It is a lonely place, infinitely peaceful.

'Look, do ye see that?' He points at an osprey rising from the loch, water dripping from a large trout it holds in its talons.

'Watch now. The osprey has a reversible front toe and it can turn the fish so that its head points in the direction of flight. It does that to reduce drag. A canny bird right enough. Aye, and a bird with odd tastes.'

'What do you mean, Grandpa?' This is the kind of information with which I can impress Jas when she comes to stay. I'd love to see her again.

'Well, Angus, the gillie hereabouts, said he found a child's teddy bear and a tartan rug in one osprey nest.'

'What a considerate parent!' I say and we laugh. But mention of a toy bear brings a bloody teddy bear to my mind, and Sandy's smashed head.

Grandpa unfolds the cloth around his ancient fly rod. The fine split bamboo takes me straight back to the island. Even here, so far away, there are so many reminders. I have to concentrate on breathing slowly.

An insect lands on my wrist, folding and unfolding its pearly peacock wings. I think of the peacock-eye tail feather I have folded into my journal, and a piece of the kite with a few of Pirsig's words: . . . *Things are better now. You can sort of tell these things.*

My illustrated journal is the only souvenir of that time apart from the gift from the monk—the tiger claw on a string, which I still wear. I haven't shown the journal to anyone. The diary of events, neglect, and actions of the twenty days we spent on Koh Tabu have not been revealed.

The curved up body of the insect tapers to whisks of long curved tail. Its front legs are speckled, its protruding eyes coloured violet. I look away and look back. It's gone.

'Grandpa, can I tell you something?'

'You can tell me anything, child.'

'You aren't to tell anyone else.'

I tell him about the gentle giant monk with his misshapen face and no tongue, how he saved my life. I tell him about his tame tiger, and how I have kept them secret from everyone all this time.

He is twisting the sections of bamboo pole together and fixing the lead and ferrule.

'You did right to say nothing, lassie. The poor fella and his beast are best let be.' We sit in companionable silence, watching the water. The osprey hovers and swoops, legs first, at the far end of the loch.

'Perhaps he has already been captured by the Khmer Rouge and killed,' I say quietly. 'Or been ill and died.'

'Perhaps, but how would you like to remember him, Bonnie?' Grandpa asks.

'Oh . . . laughing and clapping his hands, watching as the big tiger swims out powerfully. She held her head out of the water, keeping her whiskers dry.'

Grandpa smiles at me and nods.

If the monk does die, I wonder if he'll be reincarnated as a tiger, I think to myself. But I don't say it out loud.

I want to tell him about my other anxieties, things I haven't told anyone: about Hope's death and Natalie's, about Jas's dad and Layla Campbell, but I can't, not yet. Last I heard Jas's family went back to the USA along with all the other Utapao Americans I had known; there they would live, I suppose, until the next war.

'You've a wonderful way with words, Bonnie,' Grandpa interrupts my thoughts.

One day, perhaps I'll let him read my journal.

I have no idea where Layla Campbell is. I said nothing against her at the coroner's hearing. None of us did.

I wasn't exactly blameless, after all. I've had many months to dwell on my own faults.

I have made a list in my journal:

My Faults

1. *Arrogance and snobbery: I never made any attempt to get to know the Barbie Babes, because I thought they were beneath me, trashy and stupid.*

2. *Naivety: I thought that there were only good people and bad people; everything to me was black or white, right or wrong and I know now that people aren't all bad or all good, whether it's wars and politicians or husbands and wives.*
3. *I'm unforgiving, mean-spirited, pig-headed. I couldn't stand that Hope was as good at making things as me and had good ideas. I was jealous of her.*
4. *I'm bossy; always need to be in control.*

And I know that there were other things I could add to that list. Things I could hardly bear to think about.

I want to tell Grandpa that I killed Hope, or that I feel responsible for her death. And that I seriously considered deliberately letting Layla Campbell drown. And I had always thought I was so special, so clever, a good person. I thought I had Quality. But I can't tell him or anyone, not yet.

'See that, Bonnie?' He points at a fish rising at small intervals at the same place, about twenty feet away, barely disturbing the surface, occasionally baring its back fin and tail. 'That's a grand fish. There's been a mayfly hatch today. Watch now.'

I watch carefully.

'This is called dapping,' Grandpa says, as the line curves silently and straightens over his head. 'I use a large single dry fly and the hook has no barb. That way the fish won't suffer. Do you see, lassie, how I try to let nothing but the fly touch the water?'

He ties his own flies. There's an old wooden box of them on the thwart next to him, all sewn together or tied by thick fingers that look as if they could have no finesse or dexterity.

On walks he gathers any small feathers, fur, sheep's wool caught on wire, and at home he'll rummage in Grandma's sewing basket for coloured wools and silks, even glittery ribbon; anything that might make an interesting looking fly with which to fascinate a canny trout. None of them look like real mayflies, or damsels or anything the fish might usually eat, instead they are fanciful inventions, like exotic insects never found on a Scottish loch, more like insects from Koh Tabu.

The springy rod moves gracefully in Grandpa's large hands; I watch him stop it at ten o'clock, two o'clock, letting the line out then flicking his wrist; the dark water lapping; the osprey calling; a stiff breeze blurring the heather.

'It's more than just fishing, is fly-fishing, Bonnie. It's being in the middle of things that matter—wilderness like this, part of nature. Nothing like it. Blessed by the wild. Like your friend the Buddhist monk.'

I watch as a fat fish swirls and disturbs the surface and decides to take Grandpa's fly. He strikes and plays the huge fish, fighting it, reeling it in, the thin bendy rod bent almost double, and then letting it run, pulling gently on the line until it's taut, allowing it to run again, until the big old fish gradually slows its dashes. I cannot watch as it thrashes in desperation, succumbing to tiredness. My heart is pounding. Grandpa looks exhausted.

'Have the landing-net steady now. That's it. Ah! Beauty!'

It is much too heavy for me to hold. Grandpa takes it from me and removes the hook from its mouth. The huge trout is golden yellow with black and brown spots, like a leopard, and its skin holds a thousand rainbows. Its sad turned-down mouth gasps mutely. There are two other hooks buried in its lips, grown over by transparent flesh, and coloured broken lines, like a mandarin's straggly beard. It has been caught on a hook before. It has a history of battles fought and won.

Grandpa tells me to dip my hands into the loch and gives me the fish to cradle in the net, his large hands cupped around mine.

'You must never touch a trout with dry hands, you know, lassie, no, always wet your hands thoroughly.'

'Why, Grandpa?'

'It's very easy to damage their protective mucous coating, you see, and then they become sick and die.'

Another piece of information for Jas.

The trout looks but doesn't see me, its eyes staring and alien. It does not understand what it's seeing in this waterless universe. My eyes fill with tears and all I see is rainbow. Like in the poem by Elizabeth Bishop that Mum read me the other night. ' . . . until everything was rainbow, rainbow, rainbow!'

'There, you can let him go now to catch a live mayfly.'

I lean over the gunwales of the boat, dipping my arms in as far as I can, and, as Elizabeth Bishop did with *her* 'tremendous fish' let it go into the flow of the current. We sit quietly, watching as the elderly warrior swishes his tail, and hurries away, our wet hands next to each other on the thwart.

His large hand and my small one leave dark imprints on the pale wood.

Ann Kelley left her convent high school at 17, married at 18 and had two children. She is now a novelist, poet and photographer and lives on the edge of a cliff in Cornwall with her second husband and two cats. After surviving several winter disasters including being struck by lightning they now move to the town during the worst of the weather, to live next door to her daughter and grandchildren. Ann has had several books published including two poetry collections, two books of photographs, an audio book of cat stories and the novels *The Burying Beetle, Bower Bird*, and *Inchworm*. She has won several awards including the Costa Children's Book of the Year for *Bower Bird*. *Koh Tabu* is her first novel for Oxford University Press.